Charles Dickens
His Journal

Charles Dickens
His Journal

OF A JOURNEY
FROM
LONDON TO CANTERBURY
IN THE YEAR 1830

Adapted from His Works & Edited by
VINCENT TORRE

GEORGE BRAZILLER PUBLISHERS
New York

Published in the United States of America by George Braziller, Inc., New York.
Copyright © 2010 George Braziller, Inc.
Text © 2010 Vincent Torre.

For information, please address the publisher:
George Braziller, Inc.
171 Madison Avenue
New York, New York 10016

Library of Congress Cataloging-in-Publication Data
Torre, Vincent.
Charles Dickens : his journal of a journey from London to Canterbury in
the year 1830 / adapted from his works & edited by Vincent Torre.
    p. cm.
Includes bibliographical references and index.
ISBN 978-0-8076-1604-8 (alk. paper)
1. Dickens, Charles, 1812-1870—Diaries—Fiction. 2. Dickens, Charles,
1812-1870—Childhood and youth—Fiction. 3. Novelists, English—19th
century—Fiction. I. Title.
PS3570.O69C53 2010
813'.54—dc22
                    2010001405

Design © 2010 Vincent Torre.
Arranged by Rita Lascaro.
Printed and bound by Tien Wah Press (Singapore).
First edition.

IN MEMORY OF
NICHOLAS EVANGELIST
1920–1942

Staff Sergeant, United States Army Intelligence
Operation Tiger, English Channel

Editor's Introduction

*I*n my never-ceasing visits to church bazaars, flea markets, and Salvation Army depots, where used, or perhaps I should say ill-used, books are often sold for mere pennies, it has sometimes been my great good fortune to acquire items of bibliographic interest that I have unhesitatingly purchased, bargain prices or not. While it is true that many of these so-called finds proved in the end to be nothing of the sort, still my expenditures have been worthwhile in the aggregate.

Perhaps the reader will recall one of my greatest discoveries to date— the pocket notebook carried by Charles Dickens on his rambles in the streets and environs of London, in which he wrote and annotated the first draft of perhaps his most famous book, *A Christmas Carol*. In this instance, I am sorry to say, the literary world has yet to acknowledge my work in this field. Indeed, many in the highest institutions of learning express their doubts, often in unmistakable terms, that the notebook was written by Dickens at all, and call it a hoax or worse. My proofs of the authenticity of the handwriting on the ink-stained pages as being that of none other than Charles Dickens have failed to sway my detractors in their obtuse determinations.

I am pleased to announce a new discovery along these lines: to wit, a journal kept by Charles Dickens in the year 1830 when he was eighteen years of age, written not in his infamously illegible hand but in the shorthand at which he was an expert and of which, an early innovator. I am further pleased to say that as one of the world's leading authorities of shorthand writing, I instantly recognized Dickens's own hand in the journal. The persons from whom I purchased the volume must have thought a madman was acquiring the doodles of another madman, as Dickens's shorthand would probably have resembled in their eyes the scratchings of a chicken whose feet had been dipped in ink.

It is well known to those who have studied the life of the great novelist that the young Dickens served as a shorthand reporter in the courts of Bow Street and the corridors of the House of Commons. As his reportage in these venerable institutions revealed a marked similarity between the felons at the bar in Bow Street and the felonious members of the House of Commons, Dickens was sacked by *Bentley's Miscellany* and other London papers, which he served as free-lance under the pseudonym of "Boz." Just as glad to be released from a life of unrewarding work at insufficient wages, Dickens decided to chuck it all and, using his meager savings, embark on a walking journey of self-discovery from London to Canterbury.

Today, so many years after he wrote his world-famous books, we cannot help but wonder that one man could have conjured a list of characters so diverse and colorful that scarcely one human trait is repeated from one person to another, unless it is venality; his characters still live for us in his works. At the time Dickens embarked on his journey, even he was unaware of the labor that still lay before him, having shown only a modest talent for writing short comic sketches. It would be but a few brief years after his journey to Canterbury that he would achieve fame with the serial publication of *The Pickwick Papers*, which took London by storm. His fame endured and would become almost greater in America than in England: when he visited the New World, he was greeted like royalty.

Though not a trained draftsman, Dickens drew rough sketches in the journal of some of the people and places he encountered, sketches that would prove invaluable to the artists such as Cruikshank, Cattermole, Barnard, and "Phiz" commissioned to illustrate his novels. We wonder, however, that it was thought necessary to illustrate books whose prose was so full of characterization and color that the pictures now appear superfluous to modern eyes, however charming they may be.

Dickens carried in his pockets his savings in coin of the realm, which he trusted would carry him through his journey, and consoled himself

George Cruikshank

Charles Dickens
Kapetan Smjeli

ILUSTRIRAO
ROBERT STEWART SHERRIFFS

MLADOST
ZAGREB 1951

DICKENS:

NEHÉZ IDŐK
❖ ❖
KARÁCSONYI ÉNEK

RÉVAI TESTVÉREK IROD. INT. R. T.

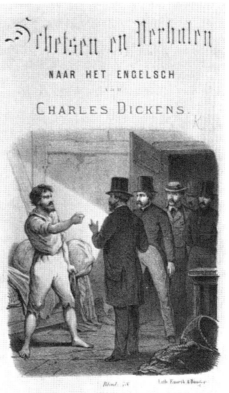

Schetsen en Verhalen

NAAR HET ENGELSCH

CHARLES DICKENS.

TE ROTTERDAM BIJ HENDRIK ALTMANN.

that, while they were heavy at the start, his pockets would be lighter each day by a few pennies. Paper currency, he knew, was not trusted by country folk—the ring of a sound shilling on a tavern table would bring a finer supper than banknotes, which were, in the eyes of suspicious rustics, probably counterfeit. Besides, paper can burn or be eaten by rats in a barn or beetles in a damp room below stairs.

And so, like Don Quixote seeking adventures, but without a trusty Rocinante to carry him when he grew footsore or a faithful Sancho Panza to act as porter and moral support, young Charles Dickens took to the road from London to Canterbury—not as Chaucer's pilgrims did, but rather, as one who follows his own star.

This "Journal," written by Charles Dickens at the age of eighteen, is, of course, imaginary. Still, we know he kept diaries; thus, a journal of a journey from London to Canterbury is a distinct possibility, as Dickens was a great walker in an age of walkers. Such a volume might very well be awaiting discovery in a dusty attic or old curiosity shop. In the meantime, there is no reason why the devotee of Dickens should be deprived of the pleasure of reading this tale of two cities in the master's own words, of which we are fortunate to possess a superabundance.

The editor, therefore, has had the temerity to *create* such a journal, with Dickens's own words supplying most of the text, gleaned from the novels in helter-skelter fashion. Writing in imitation of the master as well as he is able, the editor hopes to provide paragraphs sufficient to join, hopefully, the whole into a flowing narrative. If the editor has succeeded, he is happy; if he has failed, he apologizes to the spirit of Dickens past and to a public that has taken the time to read this fabrication.

To assure the reader that he or she is getting pure Dickens, the editor has retained all the commas, colons, and semicolons that make up so much of the typography of his novels, deleting punctuation only where deemed absolutely unnecessary, and adding a comma or two where thought absolutely necessary. It can be agreed, however, by those who love Dickens in spite of his use of excessive and inconsistent punctuation, that a great deal of the charm of his writing lies therein.

Minor changes have been made so that the journal makes literary sense. For example, Mr. Micawber calls him "My dear Dickens" instead of "My dear Copperfield." One or two changes along these lines will be evident to those who have read enough Dickens. Trotty Veck's raptures over tripe have been expanded moderately; part of Mrs. Gamp's monologue has been created by the editor; and Joe Gargery's words are almost entirely the work of the editor. All this is for better or worse, for the reader to decide. Certain descriptive paragraphs have been condensed as the beloved novelist can be wordy. In short, this imaginary journal written by Charles Dickens at the age of eighteen is presented in homage to the master, whose unassailable reputation can be neither diminished nor enhanced by such presumption.

Charles Dickens
His Journal

Prefatory Note

*H*aving attained my majority with no great expectations of an inheritance from a bankrupt and feckless father, who has spent more of his days in Marshalsea debtors' prison waiting for something to "turn up" than he ever did with his growing family; and having myself fallen on hard times, with no distinct prospect of a career by which to make my own fortune, I begin this Journal of a Journey from London to Canterbury with these few lines by way of autobiography.

To begin my life with the beginning of my life, I record that I was born (as I have been informed and believe) on a Friday, at twelve o'clock at night. It was remarked that the clock began to strike, and I began to cry, simultaneously. We arrive promptly at anno Domini 1824, when I was twelve years of age, nothing having occurred in the interim that could possibly be of interest to the inquisitive reader, save that those years were passed in relentlessly grinding hunger. At the age of twelve, so that I might contribute to a household that was intimately acquainted with

penury, I was put to work in Warren's Blacking Warehouse, Hungerford Stairs, abutting on the river and literally overrun by rats.

My work was to cover the pots of paste-blacking, first with a piece of oil paper, and then with a piece of blue paper; to tie them round with a string; and then to clip the paper close and neat, all round, until it looked as smart as a pot of ointment from an apothecary's shop. When a certain number of grosses of pots had attained this pitch of perfection, I was to paste on a label, on which was printed in distinctive fonts the name of Warren's, with a notice at the bottom of the label stating that the contents of the pot were warranted pure, and with a stern warning that the product should be sold for no less or more than five shillings and sixpence per pot. An impressive seal was affixed to the pot for the express purpose of deceiving the purchaser into believing the paste-blacking was endorsed by a high office of the government. An older boy, who was my immediate superior, baited me unmercifully as the offspring of a resident of debtors' prison, thus endowing me with the humiliating sobriquet of "Work'us." For this demeaning and dirty labour my remuneration was fourpence per diem.

I was eventually released from this bondage when my father was released from the Marshalsea, at which time he looked forward to a "new start" that never materially affected the family fortunes in the least. Perhaps a paragraph or two on debtors' prisons will prove enlightening to those who have not had the pleasure of residing in one, or never

visited one of these institutions in an hour of leisure, as so many do out of morbid curiosity.

The smallest of these prisons is the Marshalsea, in Borough High Street, near St. George's Church. In one part of the prison some solitary tenant might be seen, by the light of a feeble tallow candle, over a bundle of soiled and tattered papers, yellow with dust and dropping to pieces from age; writing, for the hundredth time, some statement of his grievances, for the perusal of a great man whose eyes it may never reach, who is begged to alleviate the sufferings of that solitary tenant. Or, a man and his wife, and a whole crowd of children, might be seen making up a scanty bed on the ground, or upon a few chairs, to pass the night in these putrescent precincts, where the mice are most at home. There is the same air about them all—a listless, jail-bird, careless swagger, wholly indescribable. The noise, the lingering odours of gin, beer, tobacco, suppers past, and unwashed inmates, only add to the airless miasma of the place.

In the galleries themselves, and more especially on the staircase, might be seen a great number of people who came there; some because their room, if they could afford to pay the Keeper for one, is empty and lonesome; more especially if they have no room at all; many because they are restless or don't know what to do with themselves in a place where there is nothing to do, and where the minutes pass more slowly than anywhere else on earth. There are

many classes of people there, from labouring men in fustian jack-ets, to the broken-down bankrupt in his dressing-gown and shawl.

When I was fifteen years of age, I received some desultory schooling, where I should learn to read and write a more or less legible script, at which I failed miserably, in order that I might undertake a position as a clerk in a bank or commercial company. I was therefore apprenticed to a Mr. Pickwick, bookseller, whose shop was called The Horace Head, Tavistock Street, Covent Garden, with a sign above the door on which was painted a crude portrait of the odist, suitable to the dignity of the establishment. I was to dust, sort, and catalogue the books and deliver volumes to Mr. Pickwick's clientele. At either side of the front door were placed, in fair weather, open bins where excessed books were sold at a shilling per volume. Gentlemen who stopped to peruse the works of Johnson and Hume were frequently relieved of their purses by the street arabs who hung about, looking for a mark. Two urchins, known to the parish beadle as "Dodger" and "Twister," particularly shone in this pro-fession. My wages in the bookshop were sixpence per diem.

Mr. Pickwick was a kindly gentleman, who had achieved a small notoriety in poetic circles with a volume of Hudibrastics written when a

young man, entitled *Leaves That Fall in Fall,* with a frontispiece portrait in mezzotint. For a labour that swallowed his youth, Mr. Pickwick had received from his publishers, whom he denounced as a pack of d----d scoundrels, a royalty of ten shillings; whereupon he gave up writing poetry forever, having determined that it was easier to sell books than to write them, consoling himself with the thought that fame was in any case tragically impermanent.

Thus it happened one afternoon that Mr. Pickwick, entering the storage room without making any discernible sound, discovered me reading Smollett when I should have been shelving the latest shipment of books. It was not the first time that Mr. Pickwick had caught me reading instead of attending to the duties of an apprentice, so I was dismissed on the spot. My wages were paid up to the moment, with a ten percent discount for furthering my education at his expense; at which I remarked that the discount should have been fifty percent, if the truth were known; whereupon Mr. Pickwick bade me good afternoon, and I bade farewell to the bookseller's trade.

From the age of seventeen to eighteen, I worked as a reporter for several of the London periodicals, using a method of shorthand I had learned at the Mechanics' Institute, and perfected for my own purposes. With my skill at shorthand, I was able to record the proceedings in the courts of Bow Street, and the procedures of the House of Commons; at times drawing no clear distinction between the crimes of highwaymen and the criminalities of gentlemen; having determined that I would record faithfully what I heard and saw, and to leave it to the reader to make his own determinations in the matter. For my unswerving endeavours in picturing the cut-throats at the bar in Bow Street, and the cut-purses of the House of Commons (who spent much of their time at another kind of bar), I was dismissed by *Bentley's Miscellany* and other papers, with the managing editor's advice that I would never be a writer if I insisted on

calling a spade a spade; and that I might just as well throw myself into the Thames and save myself from further grief. One of my revelatory articles, which got me into troubled waters with my employers, included the following passage:

"Used 'tallysticks' were housed at Westminster, and it would naturally occur to any of us unofficial personages that nothing would have been easier than to allow them to be carried away for firewood by some of the many miserable creatures in that neighbourhood. However, they never had been useful, and official routine could not endure that they should ever be useful; and so the order went forth that they should be privately and confidentially burnt. It came to pass that they were burnt

in a stove in the House of Lords. The stove, over-gorged with these preposterous sticks, set fire to the panelling of the House of Lords, the House of Lords set fire to the House of Commons, then the two Houses were reduced to ashes."

Ascertaining beyond the shadow of a doubt that I never *would* fill pots of paste-blacking, sell used books, or report for the papers with any degree of satisfaction to my employers, but must inevitably end up in the street again and again, I determined to leave London and follow the road to Canterbury—as so many others have done, to find one thing or another—not as a pilgrim, but on a pilgrimage to find myself. To put this enterprise into effect, I withdrew my savings from Cheeryble's Bank, a paltry eighteen shillings (coincidentally, my very age), which I had saved at the expense of my appetite, and which I trusted would not deplete that sound institution's reserves to such an extent as to cause a run on the bank by depressed depositors.

Eighteen shillings, I estimated, would see me through at least a fortnight of travel if I husbanded them carefully, and learned to live off the land like a soldier of the King. If perchance I were to pick up apples and other fruits from trees whose branches overhung the highway, and be told by a sly farmer that those were *his* fruits even if a branch did overhang the road, I was prepared to advise such a farmer that as it was the King's highway, and as I was a loyal subject of the King, under whose

protection I travelled that road, that the fruits belonged to whomever claimed them at first sight. In the reasonable expectation that I could easily outwit any farmer who stood between myself and a good supper, I set my plans. Thus, with map in hand, I plotted my way carefully so as not to wander off it, which would have extended my purse beyond its capabilities. I would pass through the cities and towns of Rochester, Chatham, Faversham, Whitstable, Margate, Ramsgate, Deal, Dover, Folkestone, Hythe, Ashford, with my final destination at Canterbury.

To equip myself for this expedition, I acquired the following gear: a pair of stout boots from a pawnshop, which I was assured had seen action at Waterloo and were still serviceable, at fourteen pence; a rain-proof hat to deflect the unsettled climate of the County of Kent, which, subject to the vagaries of the Channel and the North Sea, could never be safe from an unanticipated inundation; a coat and trousers of coarse material made in Scotland, which I was confident would repel any burrs or thorns I might encounter in fields and hedges; and a change of linen.

To record my adventures and *mis*adventures, I purchased a small Journal with a strong water-proof cover, and pages of the newly manufactured light-weight onion-skin paper; an experimental reservoir pen, and a two-ounce bottle of Dombey's Dissoluble India Ink. For reading matter, when rain should detain me from moving on, I acquired duodecimo volumes of Shakespeare and Sir Walter Scott set in minion type. All this I would carry on my shoulder in one of the new knapsacks made of light-weight woven material covered with India rubber.

I resolved to keep my Journal faithfully, never letting a day pass without recording what I had seen and heard: to wit, the peculiarities and nuances of speech of such persons as I might engage in conversation, no matter how trivial or exalted they may be; the impressions made upon my eye by the architecture of houses, churches, and public buildings, etc., no matter how mean or exalted *they* may be; the manners and mannerisms, and the dress and costume of all I may encounter, the rustic and the sophisticated, wherever I find them; always keeping uppermost in my thoughts Bacon's sound words of advice: "Hunt more after choiceness of phrase, and the round and clear composition of the sentence, and the sweet falling of the clauses."

I further resolved to embellish nothing for the sake of style, nor will I attempt to develop one; neither will I add nor detract from what I observe, but will avoid over-colourful description as is so often made by those seeking an immediate reputation. I will avoid prolixity even when seized by the urge to do so; will eschew intolerable mannerisms except where absolutely necessary for emphasizing my theme. I will not make a rivulet a river, or a mole-hill a mountain; will call a pig a pig, and a cow a cow. Nor will I attempt to raise a goose to Parnassus or a goat to Olympus. In short, the humdrum will be as exhilarating to me as the exalted.

I determined to leave London at an early hour on the first day of Spring, always an augury of successful ventures. I settled my accounts with my landlord, Mr. Ralph Nickleby, a money-lender who tested shillings in his teeth; with the coffee-man at whose cart I had enjoyed many a scanty breakfast; and with the oyster-man at whose stall I had relished those succulent bivalves on the rare occasions when I was in funds. On that fateful morning I will recite aloud to the empty streets of London Shakespeare's jingle appropriate for those seeking encouragement to continue in their journey:

> *Jog on, jog on the footpath way,*
> *And merrily hent the stile-a.*
> *Your glad heart tires in a day,*
> *Your sad heart in a mile-a.*

Day the First

J left London this morning at first light, in order to be well away from the city with its incessant roar of traffic, the pleading cries of beggars, the squealing of children playing in the mud, the smell, the dust—and to be fairly well into the countryside before the sun rose higher.

There is no time in the whole year in which nature wears a more beautiful appearance than in the Spring. The charms of this time of the year are enhanced by their contrast with the Winter season. We see nothing but clear skies, green fields, and sweet-smelling flowers—when the recollection of snow, and ice, and bleak winds has faded from our minds as completely as they have disappeared from the earth. And what a pleasant time of the year it is—orchards and corn-fields ring with the hum of labour; trees bend beneath the thick clusters of rich fruit that bend their boughs to the ground; the influence of the season seems to extend itself to the very waggons whose slow motion across the fields is perceptible only to the eye, but strikes with no harsh sound upon the ear.

The sun shone pleasantly on the bright brooks that were sometimes shaded by trees, and sometimes open to a wide extent of country, intersected by running streams and rich with wooded hills, cultivated land, and sheltered farms. Now and then, a village with its modest spire, thatched roofs, and gable-ends would peep out from among the trees; and more than once, a distant village, with church towers looming through its smoke, and high factories and workshops rising above the mass of houses, would come in view; and, by the length of time it lingered in the distance, showed me how slowly I travelled.

I had visions of long roads that stretched away to the horizon; of ill-paved towns, uphill and down, where faces would come to dark doors and ill-glazed windows, and where rows of mud-bespattered cows and oxen would graze; bridges, post-yards, little cemeteries with black crosses settled sideways in the grass, with wreaths upon them drooping away; again, of long roads, dragging themselves up hill and down dale, to the limitless horizon; of being unable to reckon up the hours I would spend on the road; of being parched, and giddy, and growing half-witted.

I picked up a stout branch, which I proposed to use as a staff for support should I grow footsore; and to discourage highwaymen, should I meet with any fellows of that brotherhood. The first hour or two were uneventful, save for hearing bird-songs unfamiliar to my city ears, having known only the chatter of sparrows, the cooing of pigeons, and the squawk of seagulls near the wharfs. I saw flowers that delighted my eyes,

having known only the weeds that grow in muddy lanes. A farmer sitting at his door was the first person I encountered, save for carters carrying various kinds of merchandise into the city. I greeted him with a cheery "Halloa," to which he responded with a deafening silence. I had learned in London that the best way to strike up a conversation with a stranger was to ask for directions. Thus, I enquired of the farmer if this particular road ran to Canterbury. His reply:

"Young man, you can see for yourself that this road an't runnin' nowhere. Roads don't run, as a rule. They stay where they lay and don't

do much runnin' in any direction. And roads an't pertickler, nither. No, Sir, this road don't run nowhere pertickler."

I rephrased my question by asking if this road would take me to Canterbury. His response:

"This road can't take nobody nowhere. Roads can take a lot, speshly fools that tramp on 'em. They can take a lot o' rain, too, before turnin' muddy. They can take a lot o' snow coverin' 'em deep, and still be roads underneath. When the snow melts in the Spring, they'll still be there, bein' roads as usual."

For the third time, I asked if this road goes to Canterbury. He said:

"As you can see for yourself, this road an't goin' nowhere. Roads don't go nowhere, in general. They just sets and be roads. You'll waste a lot o' your time, and other folks' time, lookin' for a road that goes somewhere."

Abandoning any further attempt to start a sensible conversation with the farmer, who I was certain was trying to make things as difficult as possible for a stranger, I asked if I might have a cup of water from his well. He replied:

"How'm I supposed to know if you might or might not have a cup of water from my well? How'm I supposed to know what you might or might not have, in any case? I don't pay no mind to what anybody might or might not have till they have it."

I transcribe this utterly exasperating conversation with the farmer, though I am unable to find words to describe the infuriating tone of his voice. I hope to do better along these lines, if I pursue the career of novelist, where characteristics of speech can tell more about a person than any mere description of his or her personal appearance. I will keep this in mind in future, and can thank the farmer for that lesson.

I walked on another mile or two after bidding the farmer good-bye, to which he responded with another deafening silence. In the distance, I noticed a group of travellers approaching slowly, appearing somewhat like a caravan. At the head of this strange parade of persons was a gentleman of sound dimensions, though not actually weighty. He had a face of no particular character, which served him well, as I was soon advised that he was an actor, and that the entire caravan consisted of a troupe of travelling thespians, with himself as director. He responded favourably to my "Halloa," and launched into the following prologue in a rather theatrical style:

"My name is Vincent Crummles, Sir. That is not to say my name is Vincent Crummles Sir. I trust you noticed a breathless pause following my surname? That pause was meant for a comma. A *Player* must

emphasize his punctuation, lest the *Audience* miscomprehend his meaning. A *Play-goer* cannot discern a colon or a semicolon, but he *will* note an unemphasized comma. You have perceived perhaps that the Bard himself uses the colon and semicolon sparingly, but employs the comma lavishly? It cannot be dispensed with. A misplaced comma can bring down *Dramatis Personae*, change the meaning of an *Act*, write *Finis* to a *Scene*. Suppose I were to cry, 'A horse, a horse, my kingdom for a horse!' without making it quite clear that there are two supremely important commas in that ejaculation. Why, the *Plot* would be lost to everyone, the *Audience* would *Exeunt,* demanding a refund of their *Tickets,* which spells *Curtains* for a *Company.* Try to imagine that deathless phrase without the commas. *Un*-imaginable, Sir! In short, never leave your commas in doubt. Have you ever trod the *Boards*?"

I explained to Mr. Crummles that I was journeying from London to Canterbury on a pilgrimage, to discover if I was meant for the life of an author. He continued:

"Ah, Sir, you remind me of myself when I was young, and eager to find my *Scenario* in the *Comedy* called LIFE! When but a lad, I was taken to see a *Show of Strolling Players* and was struck by what I saw. I knew on the spot that I would be an *Actor*, and, Sir, I have never regretted it. Nor will you, if you take up the life of the *Theatre*. Think of the experience— here today, there tomorrow; villain today, hero tomorrow; prince today, fool tomorrow. All the emotions of quotidian life are compact on the *Stage*, without having to suffer them yourself. Sir, a life in the *Theatre* is the only life, I promise you."

I replied that I enjoyed going to the theatre when I could pay for a ticket, and sometimes envisioned myself on the stage. He continued:

"One look at you tells me you were *meant* for the *Stage*. You have a fine figure enough, an imposing brow, a firm chin, a piercing eye—and as for your nose—Roman, Sir, Roman! Your voice will carry to the *Gallery*, from the sound of it. At the *Matinees* you will undoubtedly be the idol of all fair eyes in the *Boxes*. Think of the conquests, Sir, the conquests! It's all a question of *Make-up*. That you wear no facial adornments is to

your advantage. Hirsute *Properties* can be applied to your visage as occasion demands—a deceiver's curling moustache, a prophet's white beard, a poet's disordered locks, and, ah, so forth. You are admirably suited to perform in variable *Parts*. It only requires experience to build up your own *Repertoire*. Perhaps you will consider joining our happy *Troupe?*"

I said that I might be more interested in writing plays than acting in them, to which he replied:

"No better experience for *writing Plays* than *acting* in 'em! What the Bard did, you can do. You, too, will learn the art of *Play-writing* through *Play-acting*. I, myself, have written a *Farce* or two that have met with a modest success in the provinces. Nothing as fine as *Midsummer Night*, of course, though I believe I have broken new ground in this particular style. In any case, the unlettered bumpkins who come to the *Show* don't know the difference. Make 'em laugh, make 'em cry! The world is a *Stage!* The *Stage* is a world of *Entertainment!*"

I remarked that his proposal was quite exhilarating. Mr. Crummles continued:

"Allow me to introduce my better self, Mrs. Crummles, my constant companion in all the exaltations *and* lamentations that must inevitably befall those who labour in the *Theatre*; and our daughter, universally acclaimed as the 'Phenomenon.' Fortunately, our various talents at *Improvisation* have saved many a *Premiere* from disaster should the leading man *Enter Stage Left* too intoxicated to remember his *Lines*. But these are the fortunes of the *Theatre*. I see you are a sober young man who can be relied upon. How say you?"

I confessed that, after hearing Mr. Crummles' monologue on life in the theatre, I was intoxicated, indeed, and was half-inclined to join the Company on the spot. I promised to give it my deepest considerations and to look them up in London, where "The Crummles Company of Transitory Thespians" were engaged for three weeks at Astley's Theatre, if nothing better turned up. With hand-shakes all round and best wishes for the future, I took my leave of Mr. Vincent Crummles, Mrs. Crummles, the young "Phenomenon," and the entire Company, determined to follow my destiny for better or for worse, as Fate decreed.

Alone on the road again with my thoughts, I envisioned myself onstage in various parts, even if only in an amateur capacity. Perhaps I, too, would write plays, as Mr. Crummles did, and act in them, as he did. Dismissing such thoughts as fantasies, I slept that night in a windmill, with the stars and Moon as backdrop to my day-dreams, and the city of Rochester in the distance. I found myself to be in a poetic frame of mind, with the arms of the windmill creaking in the wind, so inscribed the following effusion in my Journal:

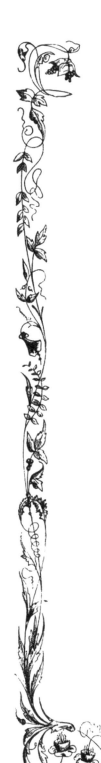

The Ivy Green

Oh, a dainty plant is the Ivy green,
That creepeth o'er ruins old!
Of right choice food are his meals I ween,
In his cell so lone and cold.
The wall must be crumbled, the stone decayed,
To pleasure his dainty whim:
And the mouldering dust that years have made
Is a merry meal for him.
  Creeping where no life is seen,
  A rare old plant is the Ivy green.

Fast he stealeth on, though he wears no wings,
And a staunch old heart has he.
How closely he twineth, how tight he clings
To his friend the huge Oak Tree!
And slily he traileth along the ground,
And his leaves he gently waves,
As he joyously hugs and crawleth round
The rich mould of dead men's graves.
  Creeping where grim death has been,
  A rare old plant is the Ivy green.

Whole ages have fled and their works decayed,
And nations have scattered been;
But the stout old Ivy shall never fade,
From its hale and hearty green.
The brave old plant in its lonely days,
Shall fatten upon the past:
For the stateliest building man can raise,
Is the Ivy's food at last.
  Creeping on, where time has been,
  A rare old plant is the Ivy green.

Private Theatricals.

COMMITTEE,

Mrs. TORRENS,
W. C. ERMATINGER, Esq.

Mrs. PERRY.
Captain TORRENS.

THE EARL OF MULGRAVE.

STAGE MANAGER—MR. CHARLES DICKENS.

QUEEN'S THEATRE, MONTREAL;

ON WEDNESDAY EVENING, MAY 25TH, 1842,

WILL BE PERFORMED,

A ROLAND FOR AN OLIVER.

MRS. SELBORNE. ———— *Mrs. Torrens*
MARIA DARLINGTON. ——— *Miss Griffin*
MRS. FIXTURE. ———— *Miss Ermatinger.*
MR. SELBORNE. ——— *Lord Mulgrave,*
ALFRED HIGHFLYER. ——— *Mr. Charles Dickens*
SIR MARK CHASE. ———— *Honourable his Matthews*
FIXTURE. ———— *Captain Willoughby.*
GAMEKEEPER. ———— *Captain Granville*

AFTER WHICH, AN INTERLUDE IN ONE SCENE, (FROM THE FRENCH,) CALLED

Past Two O'clock in the Morning.

THE STRANGER. ——— *Captain Granville*
MR. SNOBBINGTON. ——— *Mr. Charles Dickens*

TO CONCLUDE WITH THE FARCE, IN ONE ACT, ENTITLED

DEAF AS A POST.

MRS. PLUMPLEY. — *Mrs. Torrens*
AMY TEMPLETON. —— *Mrs. Charles Dickens!!!!!!!*
SOPHY WALTON. ——— *Mrs. Perry,*
SALLY MAGGS. ——— *Miss. Griffin*
CAPTAIN TEMPLETON. —— *Captain Torrens*
MR. WALTON. ——— *Captain Willoughby.*
TRISTRAM SAPPY. —— *Hon. Griffin*
CRUPPER. ——— *Lord Mulgrave*
GALLOP. ———— *Mr. Charles Dickens.*

MONTREAL, May 24, 1842.
GAZETTE OFFICE.

Day the Second

On the following morning, as I was approaching the city of Rochester, it was a harder day's journey than yesterday's, for there were long and weary hills to climb; and in journeys, as in life, it is a great deal easier to go downhill than up. However, I kept on, with unabated perseverance, and the hill has not yet lifted its face to heaven that perseverance will not gain the summit of at last.

Onward I kept, with steady purpose, and entered at length upon a wide and spacious tract of downs, with every variety of little hill and plain to change their verdant surface. Here, there shot up, almost perpendicularly, into the sky, a height so steep as to be hardly accessible to any but the sheep and goats that fed upon its sides, and there stood a mound of green, sloping and tapering off so delicately, and merging so gently into the level ground, that you could scarce define its limits.

Hills swelling above each other; and undulations, shapely and uncouth, smooth and rugged, graceful and grotesque, thrown negligently side by side, bounded the view in each direction; while frequently, with unexpected noise, there uprose from the ground a flight of crows, who, cawing and wheeling around the nearest hill, as if uncertain of their course, suddenly poised themselves upon the wing and skimmed down the long vista of some opening valley, with the speed of light itself.

Off to my left I noticed a shabby edifice whose windows were broken more often than not, whose woodwork needed paint more often than

not, and whose bricks were among the oldest I had ever seen outside of Whitechapel. A weathered sign, the worse for the indeterminate climate of Kent, proclaimed in stern letters almost too faded to decipher, that the edifice in question was called Dotheboys Hall, Academy for Young Gentlemen. I thought it would be educational, so to speak, to enquire into this institution of higher learning, as I had never attended one myself. Perhaps I might find an empty cot on the premises where I could spend the night. I rang the rusty bell that hung upon rattling chains at the gate, whereupon a boy, who seemed to be in the latest stages of death by starvation, and was clad in raiment that hadn't felt the application of a brush, and whose face and hair hadn't seen soap and water in several weeks, asked, "What name?" To which I answered appropriately; whereupon he responded, "Quite right."

From the gate to the door of this establishment was a path surrounded by a garden, or what was left of a garden, through which a brigade of dragoons might have marched, overgrown with weeds that were a sorry lot even as weeds go. The whole place appeared to have suffered the greatest neglect possible, which, I might add, went for the boy, too. The door creaked in its hinges, of course, and the hall was but a continuation of the desolate scene I had witnessed out-of-doors. I was gruffly greeted by the director of the establishment, who reluctantly introduced himself as Mr. Wackford Squeers, and asked what did I want. When I answered that I might want a bed for the night, he replied that he wasn't "running an inn."

Just then, a lady came into the library where I conversed with Mr. Squeers, and in an agitated state exclaimed:

"Drat the things! I can't find the school spoon anywhere! Isn't it brimstone and treacle this morning, Mr. Squeers?"

"I forget, my dear," replied Mr. Squeers. "Yes, it certainly is. How right you are, Mrs. Squeers. We purify the boys' blood, now and then, Mr. Dickens."

"Purify, fiddlesticks!" cried the agitated lady. "Don't think, young man [addressing herself to me], that we go to the expense of brimstone and treacle, just to purify *them* [waving her arms broadly to the academy], because if you think we carry on business in *that* way [bringing her nose closer to mine], you'll find yourself mis-*taken*."

Having delivered herself of this jeremiad, Mrs. Squeers put her hand into a closet and instituted a stricter search after the implement in question, in which Mr. Squeers and I assisted. When the solitary spoon was found at last, Mrs. Squeers, as highly agitated as ever, quit the library without uttering another word to Mr. Squeers or myself.

"A most valuable woman," confided Mr. Squeers, when we were alone. "I don't know her equal, I don't know her equal. That woman, Sir, is always the same—always the same bustling, lively, active, saving creetur that you see her now. But, come; let's go to the school-room. Here, this is our shop, Mr. Dickens. Have you considered a career in *academia*?"

The school-room was grim and dirty, with a couple of windows, whereof a tenth part might have been glass, the remainder being stopped up with old copy-books and paper. There were a couple of long, old rickety desks, cut and notched, and inked, and damaged in every possible way by generations of boys. Pens and pencils, scattered on the floor, had teeth marks in them. The ceiling was supported, like that of a barn, by cross-beams and rafters, and the walls were so stained and discoloured that it was impossible to tell whether they had ever been touched by paint or white-wash.

But the pupils—the unenviable scholars! Pale and haggard faces, lank and bony figures, children with the countenances of old men, boys of stunted growth, all crowded in view together. These were the young gentlemen attending Dotheboys Hall. Mrs. Squeers, having entered the school-room in advance, stood at one of the desks, presiding over an immense basin of brimstone and treacle, of which delicious compound she administered a large installment to each boy in succession; using for the purpose that same common wooden spoon from the closet, which widened every boy's mouth to its utmost circumference when its contents were thrust unceremoniously into that mouth.

"Just over!" said Mrs. Squeers, choking the last boy almost to death in her hurry, and tapping the crown of his head with the wooden spoon to restore him. "Look sharp!" she said, as the boy hurried from her presence with all the alacrity of a startled deer. "For what you have received may the Lord make you truly thankful."

I could not but observe how silent and unhappy all the boys were after Mrs. Squeers's generous ministrations, who seemed to take great pleasure in her office. There was none of the hearty high jinks and jocund enjoyment usually found in a school-room of normal boys; none of the boisterous badinage or mischievous mirth. The business of the morning dispatched, a few slovenly lessons were performed by Mr. Squeers, which consisted mainly of smashing a birch against the legs of desultory scholars by way of enlightenment. Education, it appeared to me, was being beaten into them rather than freely and openly given by a kind teacher.

"Now, what I want is *facts*," said Mr. Squeers, to the school-room in general. "Teach these boys nothing but facts. Facts alone are wanted in life. Plant nothing else, and root out everything else. You can only form the minds of reasoning animals upon facts; nothing else will be of any service to them. This is the principle on which I teach these boys. Stick to facts, Sir! Boy Number Twenty," continued Mr. Squeers, pointing his finger at a boy who was terrified at the sight of it, "give me your definition of a horse."

Boy Number Twenty was unable to provide the definition of a horse, having become tongue-tied on finding himself with all eyes upon him, most particularly the cold gaze of Mr. Squeers.

Mr. Squeers: "Boy Number Twenty unable to provide the definition of a horse. Make a note of it, Mrs. Squeers; make a note of it."

Mrs. Squeers made a note of it.

Mr. Squeers: "Boy Number Sixteen! Give us your definition of a horse."

Boy Number Sixteen: "Quadruped. Graminivorous. Forty teeth, namely twenty-four grinders, four eye-teeth and twelve incisive. Sheds coat in the Spring. Hoofs hard, but requiring to be shod with iron. In marshy countries sheds hoofs, too. Age known by marks in mouth."

Mr. Squeers: "Boy Number Sixteen is commended for his definition of a horse. Make a note of it, Mrs. Squeers; make a note of it."

Mrs. Squeers made a note of it.

Losing no more time than was necessary to make the school-room

appear like an institution of learning, rather than a prison, Mr. Squeers
retired to his library, where a fire crackled smartly, and where he would
soon partake of his supper, prepared by Mrs. Squeers. I was half-heartedly
invited to join them, and, though I was not tempted by nervy meat and
grey potatoes, still my hunger obliged me to accept their offering, which
tasted to me like scraps from the kitchen. I slept fitfully in the dark corner allotted to me below stairs, with the black beetles and spiders whose
domain it was. I considered myself fortunate, however, as the night
proved a chill one, and my adamant bed was warm enough.

   In the morning, the juvenile gentlemen of Dotheboys Hall were in
a mutinous frame of mind. With lingering memories of brimstone and
treacle, and the taste of it still on their tongues, they revolted as soon as
Mr. and Mrs. Squeers entered the school-room. One of the larger boys,

who was new to the academy, and hadn't yet been starved to the point where he looked as skeletal as the others, sat on their tormentors in turn, to hold them down, while other boys gave the Squeers a dose of their own medicine. Some poured a generous portion of that estimable elixir down Mrs. Squeers's throat, saying they trusted she found it satisfactory; others dealt Mr. Squeers a sound serving of the birch, asking if he approved of their method of application. Mr. and Mrs. Squeers howled in protest, of course, which only encouraged the boys to redouble their efforts. Amid the cries of glee and pain emanating from one throat or another, and the general Pandemonium of the school-room, I was exceeding glad to say farewell to Dotheboys Hall.

Day the Third

As I was approaching the town of Chatham, I saw a knot of people at the side of the road. When I drew closer to observe the proceedings, I noted a farmer or two and a gaggle of young fellows playing, at that moment, at the old shell-game with a man who was obviously a stranger to the village. I had become familiar with the shell-game in the streets of London, where many a gullible clerk was relieved of his wages in what was no game at all, as the outcome was never in doubt to the astute observer.

The man who was running the shell-game said:

"Come now, gen'l'men and lads, here's yer chance to make yer fortun'. Three shells and one little pea. With a one, two, three—and a three, two, one. Catch him who can. Look and keep yer eyes open, and niver say die! All's fair and above board. Them as don't play, can't vin. Bet, gen'l'men, any sum of money, from a farthin' to a crown. Name the shell that covers the pea, and ye've made yer fortun'."

His accomplice, of course, was a stranger like himself; but having arrived at that spot from the opposite direction, it was assumed that the two gentlemen were unknown to each other. Nothing could be further from the truth. The accomplice placed a bet on a certain shell, the pea was underneath, and he won a shilling, saying that the game was a simple one, and he had never made such easy money. The innocent country boys are easily taken in, and relieved of their few pennies. The operator of the shell-game says:

"Better luck, next time, lads. Today I vin, tomorrow you vin. Niver mind the loss of a bob or two. Ye'll have a chance to vin it back next time I come this vay."

As can readily be imagined, never again would he come that way.

While everyone was wondering how it happened that not one of them could tell where the pea was hidden, I placed my bet on the center shell, saying the pea was there; and, resting my finger firmly on the shell, requested the trickster to turn over the other two shells, which, if they proved vacant, would show that the mystifying pea *must* be under mine. I had seen a man do that in London. Of course, it could only be done once, but in that single opportunity a shilling or two could be won.

The trickster protested that the game wasn't played that way, that I should play the game "proper," if I was a "sportin' gen'l'man." I insisted there was nothing wrong with the way I played the game, and that he had only to show the pea beneath one of the other shells to win my shilling. He had no recourse but to turn over the other shells, which he was reluctant to do, until a strapping lad clenched his fists in menacing terms. I won my shilling, whereupon the trickster and his accomplice were shown the road, with a few well-placed kicks, when it was shown that there was no pea under *any* shell. With my pocket heavier by one shilling, my heart was lighter by a corresponding amount.

I entered the town, where it happened to be market-morning. There were pens in the center of a large area, filled with sheep, and tied up to posts were oxen, three or four deep. Countrymen, butchers, drovers, hawkers, boys, girls, men, women, thieves, idlers, and vagabonds, were mingled together in a dense mass; the whistling of drovers, the barking of dogs, the bellowing and plunging of oxen, the bleating of sheep, the grunting of pigs, the cries, oaths, and shouts and quarrelling on all sides; the ringing of bells, and the roar of voices; the crowding, pushing, bleating, and whooping; the hideous and discordant din that resounded from every corner of the market rendered it a stunning and bewildering scene, which quite confounded my senses.

It being election time, too, many in the crowd were carrying banners and placards on which were printed in clamorous fonts the names of their favoured candidates. Every voice tried to shout down every other voice; consequently, no ear could hear what any voice was shouting, as is so often the case at election time. The candidates, who stood on platforms safely separated by the ample aldermen of the town so they wouldn't be tempted to tweak each other's noses, were one Fizkin and one Slumkey.

Fizkin, a Tory, was tall and thin, with a pale face, and ears that stuck out; and Slumkey, a Whig, was short and stout, with a ruddy face, and ears that didn't stick out at all. Fizkin and Slumkey were haranguing the mob simultaneously, so no one could hear what either gentleman was expounding; which didn't matter at all, as everyone had already made up their minds whom they were going to vote for, and were in any case too inebriated to hear what *anyone* was saying.

The only inn of the village was The Jolly Sandboys, a structure of ancient date, with a sign representing three sandboys, increasing their jollity with just as many jugs of ale and bags of gold. The sign creaked and swung on its post on the road, with another similar sign swinging on

rusty chains over the door. It was an old building with more gable-ends than a lazy man would care to count on a sunny day; huge zigzag chimneys, out of which it seemed as though even smoke could not choose but to come in more than naturally fantastic shapes imparted to its tortuous progress. Over the doorway was an ancient porch, quaintly and grotesquely carved, and there were two grim-looking high-backed settees, which, like the twin dragons of some fairy-tale, guarded the entrance to the inn. Whole colonies of sparrows chirped and twittered in the eaves, and there were more pigeons about the stable-yard and outbuildings than anybody but the landlord could reckon up. With its overhanging stories, and front bulging out over the road, The Jolly Sandboys resembled a ship about to be launched.

I entered the inn and looked about. It was an old building, to be certain; its windows were made of diamond-pane lattices; its floors were sunken and uneven; its ceilings blackened by the hand of Time and heavy with massive beams. With the shilling in my pocket, won by outwitting the sharpers at their own game, I was of a mind to celebrate my good fortune with a hearty supper. Thus, I enquired of the landlord what might be his best ale to accompany such a repast. He answered:

"Tupence ha'penny, Sir, is the price of the Genuine Stunning. We are also well supplied with the Old Tom 549, Young Tom 360, Samson 1421, and several others, of too inferior a quality for a young gen'l'man such as yourself, I warrant."

Then, said I, drawing forth my newly-acquired shilling, I would have the Genuine Stunning, with a good head on it.

The landlord looked at me over the bar, from head to foot, with a strange smile on his face, and instead of drawing the ale, said something to his wife, who was in a small room behind the bar. She came out from behind it, and joined him in surveying me. Here we stood, all three, the landlord in his shirt-sleeves, leaning against the bar window-frame; his

wife in her apron, looking over the little half-door; and I, in some confusion, looking back at them from outside the partition. They asked me a good many questions, seeing that I was a stranger in the town, such as: what my name might be, where I might be going, where my home might be, how old I might be, how much money I might have, and lastly, how I came to find myself in The Jolly Sandboys.

Having satisfied them on all points, mainly that I was not there to rob them, they served my ale at last, though I suspect it was not the Genuine Stunning I had ordered. I deemed it best not to pursue the issue, leaving them to content themselves that they had bilked a stranger. The landlord's wife, however, opening the half-door of the bar, returned my money, bade me drink up and God-speed in my journey, when I had told them my story. Such is the generosity toward strangers one sometimes meets with in the quiet towns and villages between London and Canterbury. This custom, I suppose, dates back to the days when pilgrims were shown hospitality on their journeys, which was thought to bring good luck to the dispenser of such largesse. I was further invited to spend the night at no charge at The Jolly Sandboys, which was well-named after all; and, having supped roundly and slept soundly, I resumed my journey in the morning, with my shilling still nesting comfortably in my pocket.

Day the Fourth

*A*s I followed the road to the town of Faversham in the morning, I saw a disorganized group approaching in a rather haphazard fashion. I could make out a man, and a woman, and a parcel of small children of various sexes and ages, who they (the man and the woman) were trying to rein in whenever they (the children) wandered off the road. Indeed, the very smallest child was an infant in arms, carried by the woman. The entire entourage struggled along with their luggage, which consisted of a hodge-podge of bundles, boxes, and bags, several of which were being dragged in the dust by the children, as they (the bundles and boxes) were larger than them (the children). Every so often the entire congregation was called to a halt by the man, so everyone could pick themselves up, dust themselves off, take stock of their belongings, and call a muster of the children, so they (the parents) wouldn't lose any, as though they (the children) were soldiers on the march.

The paterfamilias, a gentleman of middle height, whose paunch preceded him by several moments, wore long tight trousers of a grey material made greyer still by the dust of the road; and a short jacket from whose pockets protruded a threadbare handkerchief, pencils that

had been chewed thoughtfully, and a well-perused packet of newspapers. On his head was a tall hat with a broad band and a narrow brim, that had not felt the application of a brush or damp cloth in a fortnight. He wore a broad-collared shirt about which his hair fell in the style of some generations past; and his fingers protruded from a tattered pair of faded gloves that I can only describe as colourless.

The materfamilias, a lady who towered above her spouse by a head, on which was a bonnet, whose singular shape, if it ever possessed a shape, was long vanished. Her dress, of a style that had yet to be named, was covered by a shawl that matched the dress in its own lack of distinction. Her shoes had once been boots, but at present consisted of soles attached to her feet by ribbons long worn down to mere threads. In her weary arms she carried the baby, a screaming, squalling, squirming, red-faced image of its father.

The progeny of this improbable parentage were clothed in a catch-as-catch-can assortment of attire that represented the highest extravagances of the past fifty years, and so resembled nothing less than a tatterdemalion company of apprentice pirates.

When this incongruous assemblage was within hearing distance, I greeted them with my usual "Halloa," and waited for events to take their course. As the very openness of the road seemed to engender a similar openness in strangers, the head of this "household," who introduced himself as one Wilkins Micawber, launched into the following confession without delay:

"I have no scruple in saying, Mr. Dickens, that I am a man who has, for some years, contended against the pressure of pecuniary difficulties. Sometimes I have risen superior to my difficulties. Sometimes my difficulties have floored me. There have been times when they have been too many for me, and I have given in, and said to Mrs. Micawber, in the words of Cato, 'Plato, thou reasonest well. It's all up now. I can fight no more.' My dear," he continued, addressing his wife, "if you will mention to Mr. Dickens what our present position is, which I have no doubt he will be interested to know, I shall look in the papers a while, and see whether anything turns up among the advertisements."

Mrs. Micawber, following her spouse's example of confiding in a stranger without reservation, launched into the following recitation of their familial tribulations without a word of preamble:

"If Mr. Micawber's creditors *will not* give him *time*, they must take the *con*-sequences, and the *sooner* they bring it to an *issue* the *better*."

I promised I would be all ears, and Mrs. Micawber proceeded:

"Mr. Micawber was induced to think, on inquiring, that there might be an opening for a man of his talent in the Medway Coal Trade. Then, as Mr. Micawber properly said, the first step to be taken clearly was to come and see the Medway. Which we came and saw. I say 'we,' Mr. Dickens, for I never *will* desert Mr. Micawber."

I uttered my admiration and approbation, saying that it was the most sensible course, under the circumstances.

"We came," said Mrs. Micawber, who I think scarcely listened to my words, "and saw the Medway. My opinion of the coal trade on that river is, that it may require talent, but that it *certainly* requires capital. *Talent* Mr. Micawber has; *capital* Mr. Micawber has not. We saw, I think, the greater part of the Medway; and that is my individual conclusion. Being so near here, Mr. Micawber was of the opinion that it would be rash not to come on and see the Cathedral. Firstly, on account of its being well worth seeing, and our never having seen it; and secondly, on account of the great probability of something turning up in a cathedral city. We have been there three days. Nothing has, as yet, turned up; and it may not surprise you, Mr. Dickens, to know that we are at present waiting for a remittance from London, to discharge our pecuniary obligations. Until the arrival of that remittance, you find us as we are, at loose ends."

Mr. Micawber, glancing up from the newspapers, nodded his head in approval, saying that the case was very clearly and succinctly put, and that he could scarcely enlarge on Mrs. Micawber's narration. Mrs. Micawber continued without pausing for breath:

"I have a conviction, Mr. Dickens, that Mr. Micawber's manners peculiarly qualify him for the Banking Business. I may argue within myself, that if I had a deposit at a banking-house, the manners of Mr. Micawber, as representing that banking-house, would inspire confidence, and must extend the connection. But if the various banking-houses refuse to avail themselves of Mr. Micawber's abilities, or receive the offer of them with con-*tumely,* what is the use of dwelling upon *that* idea? None! As to originating a Banking Business, I know that there are members of my family, who if they chose to place their money in Mr. Micawber's hands, might found an establishment of that description. But if they *do not* choose to place their money in Mr. Micawber's trustworthy hands—which they *don't*—what is the use of *that?* Again, I contend that we are no further advanced than we were before."

I expressed my sympathy for Mr. and Mrs. Micawber in their extremity; adding that I wished it were in my power to offer aid, but as I, too, found myself in straightened circumstances, there was little I could do except show my most profound appreciation of their present plight. Mrs. Micawber, scarcely taking note of my comforting comments, continued as previously:

"I will not conceal from you, Mr. Dickens, that I have long felt the Brewing Business to be particularly adapted to Mr. Micawber's abilities. Look at Scrooge and Marley! Look at Buzzfuzz, Bumble, and Brass! It is on that extensive footing that Mr. Micawber, from my own knowledge of him, is calculated to shine; and the profits, I am told, are e-*nor*-mous! But if Mr. Micawber cannot get into those firms—which decline to answer his letters, when he offers his services even in an in-*ferior* capacity—what is the use of dwelling on *that* idea? None!"

Not a bit of it, said I, understandingly. Mr. Micawber rejoined us:

"I substantiate all Mrs. Micawber has told you, my dear Dickens; and then I will, with my ill-starred family, disappear from the landscape on which we appear to be an encumbrance. For myself, the Canterbury pilgrimage has done much; imprisonment and want will soon do all that they can, with the struggle of parental poverty; et cetera. The fair land of promise lately looming on the horizon is again enveloped in impenetrable mists, and forever withdrawn from the eyes of a drifting wretch whose Doom is sealed; et cetera, et cetera. In the words of the Bard of Avon:

> *Words are easy, like the wind;*
> *Faithful friends are hard to find.*
> *Every man will be thy friend,*
> *While thou hast wherewith to spend.*
> *But if store of crowns be scant,*
> *No man will supply thy want.*

"One last word, dear Sir: annual income twenty pounds, expenditures nineteen pounds—result, prosperity; annual income twenty pounds, expenditures twenty-one pounds—result, misery! The blossom is blighted, the leaf is withered, the God of day goes down upon the dreary scene, and, in short, you are forever floored. As *I* am!"

Following this effusion, Mrs. Micawber exclaimed:

"Micawber! I have *never* deserted you, and never *will* desert you!"

"Farewell, my dear Dickens! Farewell!" said Mr. Micawber. "Every happiness and prosperity! If, in the progress of revolving years, I could persuade myself that my blighted destiny had been a warning to you, I should feel that I had not occupied my small place in existence altogether in vain. In case of anything turning up (of which I am rather confident), I shall be extremely happy if it should be in my power to improve your prospects. Dickens, farewell!"

I took my leave of the Micawber entourage, and, with daylight fast waning, I was pressed to find shelter for the night. The last I saw of them, young, old, and all in between, the Micawbers were kissing and embracing each other, wetting with their tears every cheek that was not already

drenched with same, and promising one another that something was bound to "turn up."

I aimed my step toward the coast, where the village of Whitstable offered accommodations for the night. Where the Micawbers found shelter I am unable to say. The smell of the sea-air filled my lungs with its invigorating mists, and calmed my anxiety for that unfortunate family. I looked in all directions, as far as I could stare over this wilderness, and away at the sea, but no house could I make out. When I arrived at the coastline, I saw what looked like the wreck of an old ship, that had gotten somehow turned over on its side, high and dry on the ground. On closer inspection, it proved to be a dwelling rather than a shipwreck, as smoke was rising from what appeared to be a chimney, and smoking very smartly, indeed. Summoning up my courage before this strange

structure, not knowing but it might be a den of smugglers, I knocked on a small door that was cut into its side and was greeted by a most beautiful little girl who, unaccustomed to strangers, was, I suppose, shy of them.

The strange "house" on the beach proved to be, as I suspected, the hull of an old ship that had outlasted its usefulness at sea, but was now proving its worth on land. It had been turned bottom-side-up and made into a dwelling, with windows in the shape of port-holes, which, indeed, they were, with planking added to its sides to make it as dry as it doubt-less was when sea-worthy. Thousands of barnacles had left their marks on its sides, creating a not unpleasant pattern all over it. Its owners, or whoever discovered it on the beach, did whatever was required to turn the hulk into a "snug harbour" for its present occupants. If it had been Aladdin's palace, roc's egg and all, I could not have been more charmed with the romantic idea of living in it.

It was beautifully clean inside, and as tidy as possible. There was a table, and a Dutch clock, and a chest of drawers such as sailors carry their clothing in when embarking on a voyage; and a tea-tray with a painting on it of a lady with a parasol, taking a walk with a child who was trundling a hoop. The tray was kept from tumbling down with a dog-eared copy of *The Practical Navigator* and a well-thumbed edition of the *King James Bible*. The tray, if it *had* tumbled down, would have smashed a quantity of cups and saucers and a teapot that were grouped around the books. On the walls, which were curved according to the shape of the hull, were some common coloured pictures, framed and glazed, of Scripture subjects: Abraham in red, going to sacrifice Isaac in blue; and Daniel in yellow, cast into a den of green lions. There were some hooks in the beams of the "ceiling," the use of which I could not divine then; and some lockers and boxes and conveniences of that sort, which served for seats and eked out the chairs. Suspended from the ceiling by one of the hooks was the model of a ship, with the name *Sarah Jane* painted on the stern, which, I suppose, had been the name of the very ship whose hulk now served as a house for an old seaman and his family.

The residents of this nautical dwelling were: the above-mentioned seaman, named Dan Peggotty, who had come to the end of his sailing days, and was at present a dealer of lobsters and crawfish; his sister, a very civil woman who always wears a white apron, and does the cooking and cleaning, and is called by everyone Peggotty; the beautiful little girl who answered the door; and a very ancient lady who spends most of her time sitting and knitting in a cozy corner, and bewailing her fate, named Mrs. Gummidge, who had all the appearance of a lodger. Mr. Peggotty welcomed me heartily as follows:

"Glad to see you, Sir. You'll find us rough, but you'll find us ready."

I thanked him, and replied that I was sure I should be very comfortable in such a delightful place, if he could put me up for the night, seeing as how a storm was brewing. Mr. Peggotty replied that nothing would give him and his small crew greater pleasure, whereupon Mr. Peggotty went out to wash himself in a kettleful of hot water, remarking that "cold water never would get *his* muck off." He soon returned, greatly improved in appearance; but so rubicund, that I couldn't help thinking his face had this in common with the lobsters and crawfish—that it went into the hot water very black and came out very red.

After tea, which was strong and invigorating, the door was shut tight, and all was made snug for the night, which promised to be a stormy one. To hear the wind getting up at sea, to know that the fog was creeping over the desolate dunes outside, and to look at the fire

and think that there was no house nearby but this one, and this one a boat at that, was like enchantment to me. Little Emily, for that was the name of the beautiful child, had overcome her shyness with me, and was sitting by my side upon the lowest and least of the lockers, which was just large enough for the two of us and fitted into the chimney corner.

The table was set for supper by Peggotty, who provided a clean cloth in honor of their guest, myself, I am proud to say. The supper, as was to be expected, was a sort of slumgullion in which lobsters and crawfish danced about in bubbling brine, and onions and potatoes joined in the quadrille. As we were all doing justice to this simple but hearty repast, Mrs. Gummidge launched into the following sad reflections:

"I know what I am. I know that I am a lone lorn creetur; and not only that everythink goes contrairy with me, but that I go contrairy with

everybody. Yes, I *feel* more than other people do, and I show it more. It's my misfortun'."

Mr. Peggotty said that Mrs. Gummidge should cheer up, whereupon Mrs. Gummidge continued as before:

"I an't what I could wish myself to be. I am far from it. I know what I am. My troubles has made me contrairy. I feel my troubles, and they has made me contrairy. I wish I *didn't* feel 'em, but I do. I wish I could be hardened to 'em, but I an't. I make the house uncomfortable. I don't wonder at it."

Without intending to say a word of affairs that were not my own, I burst out to Mrs. Gummidge that I, too, felt that things were going contrary with me now and then. Everyone looked at me in wonder, and Mrs. Gummidge resumed her tirade:

"I had better go into the parish house and die. I am a lone lorn creetur', and had much better not make myself contrairy here no longer. If thinks must go contrairy with me, I must go contrairy myself. Let me go contrairy in the parish house, Dan'l, and die and be a riddance."

"She's been thinkin' of the old 'un, again," said Mr. Peggotty, "drowned at sea these many years."

It was now time to retire, and I gratefully accepted my bed for the night, a small bunk such as sailors sleep in, built into the side of the hull and closed with a curtain. There I proposed to spend the night as comfortably as I could manage, consoling myself with the thought that the old hull showed no signs of leakage. Indeed, the pelting of the rain had already started, and the wind howled down the chimney, and a raindrop or two, having found their way down the chimney, hissed in the fire. To keep the fire going until everyone was fast asleep, Mr. Peggotty sat up a while, keeping *himself* awake by quietly singing some old sea chanties:

> When but a lad...................
> The weather it was stormy
> ....a girl so sweet
> 'Twas................to warm me.
> ....the sailor boy
> A bottle of rum.........ahoy, ahoy!

I could not catch every word of these chanties, but I set one down as well as I can. I tried to read a page or two of Sir Walter Scott, but without sufficient light from the fire, I was unable to do so; and, contenting myself by placing the volume under my pillow, I fell asleep at last beneath the warmest blankets, and enjoyed a sweeter sleep than I had known thus far in my journey.

By the next morning, the storm had abated; and when I peeped my head out of the curtain, everyone was already bustling about and Peggotty was putting breakfast on the table. She wished me a good morning and trusted I slept well enough, what with the wind "howling so." I assured her I had slept very well indeed, in spite of the wind. The fire was blazing away again, thanks to Mr. Peggotty's constant concern for his little "crew" and his guest. In honor of that guest, myself, I am proud to say once more, Mr. Peggotty did not go out as usual to tend his traps and pots, saying, "they'll keep." After a breakfast of warm butter and hard biscuits, hot tea and cold kippers, I made my farewells to all, adding a word of comfort to Mrs. Gummidge, who was pleased to learn that she was not the only person in the world with whom things went contrary. Peggotty had tears in her eyes when I thanked her for the hospitality I had enjoyed in their delightful "ship-house," and Mr. Peggotty gave me a powerful hug, man to man, that my ribs will not soon forget.

When I quitted the house with my knapsack and staff, little Emily walked a way with me along the dunes until it was time for her to turn back. I remarked that she was doubtless quite a sailor, upon which she said:

"No, I'm afraid of the sea. It's been very cruel to some of our men. I have seen it tear a boat as big as our house to pieces, and drown all the men."

I asked if she would like to be a lady.

"Yes," she answered, "I should like to very much. We would all be gentle-folks together, then, me, and Peggotty, and Uncle Dan and Mrs. Gummidge. We wouldn't mind then, when there come stormy weather. Not for our own sakes, I mean. We would for the poor fishermen's, to be sure, and we'd help them with money when they come to hurt. That's why I should like to be a lady."

I said that was a very commendable thing to hear from so young a girl; but I didn't say that she had just stolen my heart. On parting, at last, she kissed me tenderly on the cheek, and I'm certain my cheek will never forget that kiss.

Day the Fifth

$\mathscr{I}$ continued along the shore after waving good-bye to little Emily, enjoying the sea-breezes and the salty smell of the sea. How many miles I travelled I cannot guess, as walking on shifting sand provides less solid footing than a well-travelled road; and though one feels as though one has travelled a great distance, it proves in the end to be not so far after all. At length I arrived at a small village somewhere between Whitstable and Margate; a sea-side settlement of non-descript fishing shacks and weathered houses.

It was by now late in the afternoon, with a mackerel gale menacing from the southeast looking as cold as the previous night. I thought of where I might spend that night in comfort and safety, as each succeeding wave shattered itself against the shore. One or two little houses, with the notice "Lodgings For Travellers" hanging, had tempted me; but I was reluctant to spend the few shillings I still possessed, and looked about for a tavern where cheaper, albeit rougher, accommodations were to be found.

It was not a time for those who could by any means get light and warmth to face the fury of weather that promised to be as stormy as the night before. Indeed, as I learned later that evening, storms were common in that locale, with seldom a day of pure sunshine providing a respite for the hardy inhabitants. I spied a tavern or inn in the offing, which looked as though it had weathered successfully many a storm, and directed my footsteps toward it accordingly.

I entered the tavern, which was called the Maypole, as advertised on the old sign that creaked in the approaching gale. Guests were crowded around the fire, congratulating themselves, as I did, on their luck in finding such a warm and delightful place, with the wind growing angrier by the minute. Each tavern on the sea-side has its group of uncouth regulars, who talk of vessels foundering at sea; of the loss of all hands on the rocks; of ship-wreck and burning thirst beneath a scorching southern sun; and of cannibal islands where one might face a fate worse than death. The fierce wind howling out-of-doors, and great puffs of strong evil-smelling tobacco only added to the horror of their tales.

The profusion, the rich and lavish bounty of the Maypole! It was not enough that one fire roared and sparkled on its spacious hearth; it was not enough that one red curtain shut the wild evening out, and shed its cheerful influence on the dining room. In every sauce-pan lid, and candle-stick, and vessel of copper, brass, or tin that hung upon the walls, were reflections of countless ruddy hangings, flashing and gleaming with every flicker of the blaze, and offering, let the eye wander where it might, interminable vistas of the same rich colour. The old oak wainscoting, the beams, the chairs, the seats, reflected the hue in a deep dull glimmer. There were fires and red curtains in the very eyes of the drinkers, in their buttons, in their ale, in the pipes they smoked.

The dining room was so very warm, the smell of tobacco so very strong, and the fire so very soothing, that by degrees I began to doze in my chair. Half-asleep and half-awake, and drowsy as a kitten, with my collar drawn up around my ears, I could not but hear the conversation of the denizens of the tavern, most of whom were local seamen, dressed in their oil-skins, as though they had come directly to the tavern from their boats, still wet on the outside, and very eager to wet themselves on the inside.

"That lad's dropped off," said one.

"Fast as a top," said a second.

"Do you hear it?" said a third. "It's enough to carry a man off his legs. It blows great guns, indeed. There'll be many a shingle blowed away tonight, and sign-boards, too, I shouldn't wonder."

"It won't break anything in Maypole," responded the landlord, gruffly. "Let it try. I give it leave. What's that?"

"The wind," answered a fourth. "It's howlin' like a banshee, and likely will all night."

"He's sleepin' uncommon hard," said a fifth, motioning, I didn't doubt, to myself.

"If he don't come to in five minutes," said the landlord, as gruffly as ever, "he'll get no supper. I shall serve supper without him. I don't serve all night, I don't! Maypole closes at eleven sharp, it does!"

I leaped from my chair and joined the other guests. I was not at all surprised to see that the supper consisted of another slumgullion, as fish of all kinds were easy to catch in the area, and pigs scarcer than pearls in the desert. For my part, I swallowed the mess with as much bread as possible, and drowned the fish for a second time with as much good ale as I could afford to pay for. As it was the only supper I would get that night, it was therefore a splendid one.

The seamen broke into song, which I supposed was some sort of sea chanty:

> *We won't go home till mornin',*
> *We won't go home till mornin',*
> *We won't go home till mornin',*
> *Till daylight doth appear.*

Just then, a young man burst through the door of the tavern with a raven, a pet I supposed, in a basket on his back. The raven and the young man were dripping from the storm. The young man said to the landlord:

"We have been afield, father—leaping ditches, scrambling through hedges, running down steep banks, up and away, and hurrying home. The wind has been blowing, the rushes and young plants bowing to it, lest it should do them harm, the cowards. And Grip, ha, ha, ha—brave Grip, who cares for nothing, and when the wind rolls him over in the dust, turns manfully to bite it. Grip, bold Grip, has quarrelled with every little bowing twig, thinking, he told me, that it mocked him, and has worried it like a bullfrog! Ha, ha, ha!"

The raven, in his little basket on his master's back, hearing the frequent mention of his name, in a tone of exultation expressed his sympathy by crowing like a cock; and afterwards running over his various phrases of speech with such rapidity and in so many varieties of hoarseness that they sounded like the murmurs of a crowd of people.

"He takes such care of me, besides, father," said Barnaby, for such was the young man's name, "such care. He watches all the time I sleep, and when I shut my eyes and make believe to slumber, he practices new learning softly; but he keeps his eye on me the while; and if he sees me laugh, though never so little, he stops directly. He won't surprise me till he's perfect."

The raven crowed again in a rapturous manner that plainly said, "Those are certainly some of my characteristics, and I glory in them." In the meantime, Barnaby came to the fire-place and prepared to eat his supper.

"He flaps his wings," said Barnaby "as if there were strangers here; but Grip is wiser than to fancy that. Jump, then!"

Accepting this invitation with a dignity peculiar to himself, the bird hopped up on his master's shoulder, from that to his extended hand, and then to the ground. Barnaby unstrapped the basket and put it down in a corner with the door open. Grip's first care was to shut it down with all possible dispatch, and then to stand upon it, believing, no doubt, that he had now rendered it utterly impossible, and beyond the power of mortal man, to shut him up in it any more. He drew a great many corks from bottles of ale, and uttered a corresponding number of hurrahs.

The landlord said it was time for his son to go to bed, whereupon Barnaby cried:

"To bed! I don't like bed. I like to lie before the fire, watching the prospects in the burning coals—the rivers, the hills, and dells, in the deep, red sunset, and the wild faces. Grip has eaten nothing since broad noon. To supper, Grip! To supper, lad!"

The raven flapped his wings, and, croaking in his satisfaction, hopped to the feet of his master, and there held his bill open, ready for snapping up such lumps of fish as he should throw him. Of these he received about a score in rapid succession, without the smallest discomposure.

"That's all," said Barnaby.

"More!" cried Grip. "More! I'm a Devil."

My bed for the night was a settle, which was as hard as nails; but with howling wind and waves fairly breaking on the front door of the tavern, I counted myself fortunate to have discovered a second snug harbour for the night. Still, I was unable to sleep, not merely from the tumultuous storm without, and the obdurate settle within, but from the exciting events of the day. I opened my Shakespeare at random, thinking a page or two of the Bard would put me to sleep, as he has so many school-children, who were not yet ready for *Julius Caesar* or *Timon of Athens*; and fell upon the following speech of Falstaff in *Henry IV, Part I*, which struck me so forcibly that I copied it down in my Journal by the light of the smouldering fire, as follows:

If I be not ashamed of my soldiers, I am a soused gurnet. I have misused the king's press damnably. I have got, in exchange of a hundred and fifty soldiers, three hundred and odd pounds. I press me none but good householders, yeomen's sons; inquire me out contracted bachelors, such as had been asked twice on the banns; such a commodity of warm slaves, as had as lieve hear the devil as a drum; such as fear the report of a caliver worse than a struck fowl or a hurt wild-duck. I pressed me none but such toasts-and-butter, with hearts in their bellies no bigger than pins' heads, and they have bought out their services; and now my whole charge consists of ancients, corporals, lieutenants, gentlemen of companies, slaves as ragged as Lazarus in the painted cloth, where the glutton's dogs licked his sores; and such as indeed were never soldiers, but discarded unjust serving-men, younger sons to younger brothers, revolted tapsters and ostlers trade-fallen, the cankers of a calm world and a long peace, ten times more dishonourable ragged than an old faced ancient: and such have I, to fill up the rooms of them that have bought out their services, that you would think that I had a hundred and fifty tattered prodigals lately come from swine-keeping, from eating draff and husks. A mad fellow met me on the way and told me I had unloaded all the gibbets and pressed the dead bodies. No eye hath seen such scarecrows. I'll not march through Coventry with them, that's flat: nay, and the villains march wide betwixt the legs, as if they had gyves on; for indeed I had the most of them out of prison. There's but a shirt and a half in all my company; and the half shirt is two napkins tacked together and thrown over the shoulders like an herald's coat without sleeves; and the shirt, to say the truth, stolen from my host at Saint Alban's, or the red-nose innkeeper of Daventry. But that's all one; they'll find linen enough on every hedge.

I wondered if one day I might write as vigorously and sweepingly as Shakespeare, and if I might become an actor capable of speaking such lines, not merely to his glory, but to mine, and fell asleep at last.

Day the Sixth

*N*ext morning was a fresh one, the storm having calmed in the small hours of the night. I decided I had had enough of rough seas and shifting sands, so took the nearest road leading to Ramsgate. Whether I was pressed by thoughts that the fury of the storm had heated and stimulated into a quicker current, or was merely impelled by some strong motive to reach my journey's end, on I marched, more like a hunted phantom than a man. Nor did I check my pace, until I arrived at a cross-road, down which a horseman was coming towards me, who, had he not well-nigh pulled in his horse upon its haunches, nearly trod me under the horse's hooves. Taking me for a highwayman, the rider said:

"Is this some scheme for robbing me? I know these roads, Sir. When I travel them, I carry nothing but a few shillings, and not a crown's worth of them. I tell you plainly, to save us both trouble, there's nothing to be got from me but a pretty stout arm, considering my years, and this tool, which, mayhap from long acquaintance with it, I can use pretty briskly. Did you never see a locksmith before, I hope? You shall not have it all your own way, I promise you, if you play at that game."

I protested that I was no highwayman, but a traveller on his way to Canterbury. A looker-on witnessed the scene, a round, red-faced, sturdy yeoman, with a double chin, and a voice husky with good living, good sleeping, good humour, and good health. He was past the prime of life, but Father Time is not always a hard parent, and, though he tarries for

none of his children, often lays his hand on those who have used him well; making them old men and women inexorably enough, but leaving their hearts and spirits young and in full vigour. Every wrinkle on the yeoman's face was a notch in the quiet calendar of a well-spent life. Although muffled up in divers coats and handkerchiefs, one of which passed over his crown, and, tied in a convenient crease of his double chin, secured his three-cornered hat, there was no disguising his plump and comfortable figure; neither did certain dirty finger-marks upon his face give it any other than an odd and comical expression, through which his natural good humour shone with undiminished lustre.

"He's not hurt," said the looker-on, referring to me. "My eyes have seen more light than yours, but I wouldn't change with you."

"What do you mean?" asked the locksmith.

"Mean? I could have told you he wasn't hurt five minutes ago. Ride forward at a gentler pace, and good-day," said the yeoman.

Finding that any further talk would only end in a personal struggle with the yeoman, an antagonist by no means to be despised, the locksmith threw back his coat, and dismounting from his horse, looked steadily at the yeoman.

Perhaps two men more powerfully contrasted never opposed each other before, face-to-face. The pale features of the locksmith set off the expressive ruddiness of the yeoman, and he looked like a bloodless ghost, while the moisture, which hard riding had brought out upon his skin, hung there in dark and heavy drops, like dews of agony and death. The countenance of the locksmith was lighted up with the smile of one expecting to detect in the unpromising stranger some latent roguery of eye or lip, which should reveal a familiar person in an arch disguise.

The face of the yeoman, sullen and fierce, but shrinking, too, was that of a man who stood at bay; while his firmly-closed jaw, his puckered mouth, and more than all, a certain stealthy motion of the hand within his breast, seemed to announce a desperate purpose very foreign to acting or child's play. Thus they regarded each other for some time, in silence.

"Humph," said the locksmith, "I don't know you."

"Don't desire to," replied the yeoman. "It's not my wish. My humour is to be avoided."

"Well," said the locksmith bluntly, "I think you'll have your humour."

With that, the locksmith whipped on his horse and rode away; at first splashing heavily through the mire at a smart trot, but gradually increasing in speed until the sound of his horse's hooves died away upon the wind; then was again hurrying on at the same furious gallop, as when he almost trampled me down.

"What in the name of wonder can this fellow be? A madman? If he had not scoured off so fast, we'd have seen who was in most danger, he or I. My stars! A pretty brag this, to a stout man. Pooh, pooh!"

Thus spoke the yeoman, bringing an end to this episode by the road, concerning myself, a locksmith, and a yeoman; an episode of breathless intensity and realistic vigour, and, I hope, an element of freshness.

Continuing down the road, with the thought that a serious confrontation had come to a happy ending, I spied something that looked like a shabby, dingy, dusty cart, which was in reality a smart little house upon wheels, with white dimity curtains festooning the windows, and window-shutters of green picked out with panels of a startling red, in which happily-contrasted colours caused the whole concern to shine brilliantly.

Neither was it a poor caravan drawn by a single donkey or emaciated horse, for a pair of horses in pretty good condition were released from the shafts and grazing on the frowzy grass. Nor was it a gypsy caravan, for at the open door, graced with a bright brass knocker, sat a Christian lady, stout and comfortable to look upon, who wore a large bonnet trembling with bows. And that it was not an unimproved or destitute caravan, was clear from this lady's occupation, which was the very pleasant and refreshing one of taking tea.

The tea-things, including a bottle of rather inviting character, and a cold knuckle of ham, were set forth upon a drum, covered with a white napkin; and there, as if at the most convenient round-table in all the world, sat this roving lady, taking her tea and enjoying the prospect. Before I had an opportunity to ask if that was the road to Canterbury, or shouting my customary "Halloa," she called out:

"Hey! Yes, you, Sir, to be sure. Who won the Helter Skelter Plate?"

I confessed to the lady of the caravan that I was regrettably ignorant of who won the Helter Skelter Plate, or even, for that matter, what a Helter Skelter Plate was.

"Don't know!" replied the lady. "Why, you was there. I saw you with my own eyes."

I confessed to the lady of the caravan that she had the advantage of me; and that whereas she might have seen *me* with her own eyes, I did not remember seeing *her* with mine. Perhaps she did see me in the village, said I, as I certainly had been there, and heard there was going to be a race that afternoon.

"Well, that's that! I suppose I never will know who won the Helter Skelter Plate. Isn't it just the way? Going to Canterbury, are you, Sir? If you don't mind a ride in a rumbunctious caravan, I can carry you a mile or two before I must turn off. Have some tea."

I said I would be grateful for a "lift" in any kind of vehicle, as I was rather footsore at the moment. When we had travelled a short distance,

I ventured to take a look round the caravan and observed it more closely. One-half of it was carpeted, and so partitioned off at the farther end as to accommodate a sleeping-place, constructed after the fashion of a berth onboard a ship, like the bunks in Mr. Peggotty's ship-house, and shaded like the little windows in vessels; though by what kind of gymnastic exercise the lady of the caravan ever contrived to get into it, was an unfathomable mystery.

The other half served for a kitchen, and was fitted up with a stove whose small chimney passed through the roof. It held also a closet or larder, several chests, a great pitcher of water, and a few cooking-utensils and articles of crockery. These latter necessaries hung upon the walls, with musical instruments such as flutes and tambourines, all of which, with the swaying of the caravan, produced a din of clanking, banging, and rattling in a cacophony fit to jangle the nerves of all but the strongest man.

"Well, Sir, how do you like this way of travelling?" asked the lady of the caravan, to the horses, I think, as she was gazing down upon their backs at the very moment she asked this question.

Surmising that her question probably had been directed at me, after all, I answered that it was pleasant indeed, for all the jostling to one's bones, and that it was a unique way of seeing the country, in spite of that. I said that if I ever possessed the necessary funds, I certainly would acquire a caravan of my own, and would get used to the pain after a while.

"Here, read that," said the lady of the caravan, pointing her arm outward and toward one side of the caravan. I did as requested and read the words **Jarley's Waxworks**, in large, ornate capitals, trimmed with gold, painted there.

"That's me, I am Mrs. Jarley," she continued; whereupon she unrolled a scroll on which was written in various fonts, **One Hundred Figures the Full Size of Life**, and, **The Only Stupendous Collection of Real Waxworks in the World**, and, finally, **Jarley's Unrivalled Collection Patronized by Nobility and Gentry and the Royal Family**. She then began to sing words of her own composition, so she said, to the tune of "If I Had A Donkey":

> *If I know'd a donkey wot wouldn't go*
> *To see Mrs. Jarley's Waxworks Show,*
> *Do you think I'd acknowledge him?*
> *Oh, no!*
> > *Then run to Jarley's Waxworks!*

I confessed that I had never been to a waxworks show, but that it must be a funny thing to see, like Punch and Judy; at which she cried out in a passion:

"It isn't funny at all! It's calm, and—what's the word again— critical?—no, classical, that's it—it is calm and classical. No low beatings and knockings about, no joking and squeakings, like your precious Punch and Judy's; but always the same, with a constant unchanging air of coldness and gentility; and so like life, that if waxworks only spoke and walked about, you'd hardly know the difference. I won't go so far as to say I've seen waxworks quite like life, but I've certainly seen some life that was exactly like waxworks."

At length we arrived at a cross-road, at which junction Mrs. Jarley and I parted company; she going one way, and I another; as it is difficult, if not impossible, for two people to ride together who are going their separate ways.

Day the Seventh

When I had travelled a short distance from the cross-road where Mrs. Jarley and I parted company, I could see in the near distance the village of Deal. The night, which I had passed in an abandoned hayloft, had been very wet, and large puddles of rain-water had gathered on the road. There appeared to be few houses in the outskirts of the village, except an old country church with a cemetery and a well. I was exceedingly thirsty, and was thus more interested in the well than the ancient gravestones that were scattered throughout the cemetery. At the door of the church was an old sexton, whom I greeted not with my usual cheery "Halloa," but with a more reserved tone of voice, as we were at the entrance of a sacred edifice. I asked the sexton if I might have a cup of water from his well, whereupon he answered:

"There's an old well there, right underneath the belfry; a deep, dark, echoing well. Forty years ago, you had only to let down the bucket till the first knot in the rope was free of the windlass, and you'd hear it splashing in the cold, dull water. By little and little, the water fell away, so that in ten years after that, a second knot was made, and you must unwind so much rope, or the bucket would swing light and empty at the end. In ten years more, the well dried up; and now, if you lower the bucket until your arms are tired, and let out nearly all the rope, you'll hear it, of a sudden, clanking and rattling on the ground below; with a sound of being so deep and so far down, that your heart leaps into your mouth, and you start away as if you were falling in."

I exclaimed that it would be dreadful, indeed, to come on such a place in the dark, as I followed his words and his dark visage. The sexton continued:

"What is it but a grave! What else! And which of our old folks, knowing all this, think, as the Spring subsides, of their own failing strength, and lessening life? Not me!"

I asked if he was very old himself, to which he answered:

"I shall be seventy-nine, next Summer."

I enquired if he still worked when he was able:

"Work? To be sure," he replied. "You shall see my gardens here about. Look at that window there. I made, and have kept, that plot of ground entirely with my own hands. By his time next year I shall hardly see

the sky, the boughs will have grown so thick. I have my written work at night, besides."

I said I admired his work, to which he continued in the same vein for some time, until he tired himself with his own recollections. I did not drink of the well-water, believing it was impure, and quit the place to continue my journey. The clouds were growing dark and I had to consider where I would spend the night. I asked the sexton where I might find shelter, perhaps a tavern or inn, or a friendly house where strangers are treated with kindness. I followed his directions and found an inn.

The yard of the inn presented all the bustle and activity which are the usual characteristics of a large coach inn. Three or four lumbering waggons, each with a pile of goods beneath its ample canopy, were stowed in the open space. Others were stowed away beneath a lofty roof which extended over one end of the yard; and others, which were probably to commence their journeys that morning, were also drawn out into the open space. A double tier of bedroom galleries, with old clumsy balustrades, ran around two sides of the straggling area and hung over the door leading to the bar and coffee-room. In the lower windows, which were decorated with curtains of saffron hue, dangled two or three printed cards, bearing references to Devonshire cyder and Dantzic wine; while a large black board announced in white letters that there were five hundred barrels of double stout in the cellars of the establishment for thirsty patrons. When I add that the weather-beaten sign-board bore the semblance of a magpie observing the public warily,

I have said all I need to say about the exterior of the edifice. I asked the "boots" if many people were stopping there just then, and if it was pretty busy. He said:

"Oh, wery well, Sir. We shan't be bankrupts, and we shan't make our fortun's; and we eats our biled mutton without capers, and don't care for horse-radish when we can get beef. There's a wooden leg in number six; there's a pair o' Hessians in number thirteen; there's two pair o' halves in the commercial; there's these here painted tops in the snuggery inside the bar; and five more tops in the coffee-room; there's a pair o' Wellinton's a good deal worn; and a pair o' lady's shoes in number five. Yes, Sir; we are wery well here."

When I remarked that it was a curious old inn, he said:

"If you'd sent word you was comin', we'd ha' had it repaired."

Seeing that the boots was well-supplied with ready retorts to all my queries, and with no desire to be baited any longer on similar lines, I prepared to enter the inn. But first I asked if he had always been a boots, to which I received a less insolent response:

"I worn't always a boots, Sir. I was a vagginer's boy, once. I was a carrier's boy at startin'; then a helper, then a boots. I'll soon be a gen'l'man's servant. I shall be a gen'l'man myself, one o' these days; perhaps with a pipe in my mouth, and a summer-house in the back garden. *I* shouldn't be surprised, for one."

When I remarked that he was quite a philosopher, he continued:

"It runs in the family, I believe, Sir. My father's wery much in that line, now. If my mother-in-law blows him up, he whistles. She flies in a passion and breaks his pipe; he steps out, and gets another. Then she screams wery loud, and falls into 'sterics; and he smokes wery comf'tably till she comes again. That's philosophy, Sir, an't it?"

I remarked that it was a fairly good substitute for it at any rate. When I asked what the name of the inn was, he replied:

"The name of the inn is Westgate House, Sir; and *my* name is Samuel Weller, as my father, likewise named Weller, christened me. Though he calls me Samivel, or Sammy, while everyone else calls me Sam, if you please, Sir."

I said "Sam" it shall be, if we meet again.

Westgate House proved to be too costly for my light pockets, so I left the premises, and a boots whose like I never expected to find again; and took myself back on the road. I dined from my knapsack on a small loaf of bread and piece of cheese; and with fresh cold water from a brook, ate heartily, and fell asleep beneath a tree next to that same brook, reflecting on Mr. Samuel—pardon me—Sam Weller's philosophical discourse.

Day the Eighth

The sun shone warmingly next day, on the bright brook whose waters had been part of my supper and were now part of my breakfast; and on the tree beneath which I slept more peacefully than I would have at a noisy inn. I woke refreshed and wrote in my Journal as I looked upon a wide extent of country, intersected by running streams and rich with wooded hills, cultivated land, and sheltered farms. Now and then, a village with its modest spire, thatched roofs, and gable-ends, would peep out from among the trees; and an even more distant village looming through the smoke of high factories and workshops, which by the length of time it lingered in the distance, showed me how slowly I travelled.

The road to Dover was pleasant enough, lying between beautiful pastures and fields, about which, poised in the sky, a lark trilled out her happy song to the new day. The air came laden with the fragrance it caught upon its way, and the bees, upborne on its scented breath, hummed forth their drowsy satisfaction as they floated by. I was now in open country; the houses were very few and scattered at long intervals, often miles apart; occasionally, I came upon a cluster of poor cottages, none with a chair or low board put across the open door to keep the scrambling children from the road, while all the family were working in the fields.

These were often the common cement of a little village; and after an interval came a wheelwright's shed or perhaps a blacksmith's forge; then a thriving farm with sleepy cows lying about the yard, and horses peering over the low wall at the passerby. There were dull pigs, too, turning up the ground in search of dainty food, and grunting their monotonous grumblings as they prowled about; plump pigeons skimming around the roof or strutting on the eaves; and ducks and geese, far more graceful in their own conceit, waddling awkwardly about a pond or sailing glibly on its surface.

The farmyard passed, then came a little inn; then the lawyer's house and the parson's rectory, at whose dread names the beer-shop trembled; the church then peeped out modestly from a clump of trees; then there were a few more cottages; then came the trim-hedged fields on either hand, and the open road again.

"God save you, Master," said an old man who was sitting on a bench outside his cottage. "Are you travelling far?"

I replied courteously that I still had a long way to go.

"From London?" he asked.

I said certainly, from London. He continued:

"Ah, I've been to London many a time. I used to go there often, once, with waggons. It's nigh two-and-thirty year since I was there last, and I hear there are great changes. Like enough! Sit thee down, Master, in the elbow chair."

I did as I was bidden, grateful for a chance to rest and cool down from my walking. He continued:

"Take a pinch out o' that box; I don't take much myself, for it comes dear, and I find it wakes me up sometimes; but you're a boy to me. I should have a son pretty nigh as old as you, if he had lived, but they listed him for a soljer. He come back home, though, for all he had but one poor leg. He always said he'd be buried near the sun-dial he used to climb upon when he was a baby, did my poor boy, and his words come true. You can see the place with your own eyes; we've kept the turf up, ever since."

His grand-daughter, a pretty girl with yellow curls, came out and handed us a cup of cool milk, which was a most refreshing and welcome addition to my poor diet. I thanked her as a gentleman would a fine lady, at which she was very pleased. I could not help but glance into the cottage. The furniture was very homely, of course: a few rough chairs and a table; a corner cupboard with a little stock of crockery and Delft; a gaudy tea-tray, representing a lady in bright red, walking *without* a parasol; a few common coloured prints on the wall and chimney; an old dwarf clothes-press, and an eight-day clock; with a few bright saucepans and a kettle comprising the whole. But everything was clean and neat, with a tranquil air of comfort and contentment.

When I finished my cup of milk, I asked how far it was to the next town or village, protesting that I must be on my way. The old man replied:

"A matter of a good five mile, Master; but you're not going on? There's a good barn hard by and you're welcome to spend the night there if you don't mind the pigs. Many a night I snored so loud myself, that my good wife, bless her mem'ry, sent me out to sleep there, sayin' she was confident I wouldn't pother the pigs."

As the weather was mild, with no sign of rain or storm, I said I would be quite comfortable in a field, and that as I too snored, at least I wouldn't "pother" the pigs. The old man laughed at my remark, nearly falling back from his chair. I thanked his grand-daughter for the milk and gave her a ha'penny, at which both she and her grand-father were mightily pleased.

When I arrived in the next small village, I saw a woman of indeterminate age tending her garden. I gave my customary cheery "Halloa," and enquired if I was on the right road to Canterbury, whereupon she replied:

"Bless my soul, a rayal gentleman! Sir, you are on the right road to Canterbury, as it says there on the road-sign, if that's where you want t' go."

I explained away my not seeing the road-sign by saying I was distracted by her beautiful garden. I realized that I would have a lot to enter into my Journal when I noticed she was watering her weeds. I questioned her on this, to which she replied:

"Bless my soul, Sir; weeds is part o' God's creation, an't they? Would ye have them be thirsty? They an't as pretty as daisies or roses, to be sure, but they be deservin' of God's good water as any o' them. Mr. Gamp, my 'usbant, run off these twenty years, Lor' bless 'im, used to water the weeds, and so will I, to 'onor 'is mem'ry. He smoked 'em, too, when tabacky was dear. Smelled awful, them weeds did, but as it pleased 'im, it pleased me. I had to hopen the winders and doors even on cold days to let out the smoke and the stink. That's all past, now, and what of it?"

Mrs. Gamp, as I supposed her name to be, in spite of her husband having run off these twenty years, solaced herself after these reflections with a pinch of snuff, and continued her monologue:

"What do ye say to a bit o' pickled salmon, with a nice little sprig o' fennel, and a sprinklin' o' white pepper? It takes new bread with just a pat o' butter, and a mossel o' cheese. I'm very partial to cowcumbers, as they do a world o' good in a sick-room. I take the Brighton Old Tipper at night, it bein' considered medic'nal by the doctors. As to gin and water, I never take a drop beyond what's considered beneficial to the consti-*tooshun.*"

She paused to sprinkle salt on her cucumber before proceeding:

"Ah, Sir, what a blessed thing it is, livin' in a wale; to be contented! I don't believe a finer cowcumber was ever growed. I'm sure *I* never seen one."

I agreed that the cucumber was indeed a very fine one and never expected to taste a better. Without a word of preamble, she began to recite the following in a sing-song manner:

> *Thrown on the wide world, doomed to wander and roam,*
> *Bereft of his parents, bereft of a home;*
> *A stranger to something, and what's his name joy,*
> *Behold little Edmond, the poor peasant boy.*

I could not make heads or tales of this verse, but write it down as well as I can remember, and make no excuse for it.

Further commenting on the cucumbers that grew in her garden, I suggested that she might consider going into the pickling business, and selling them door-to-door. As her business grew, as I was certain it must with such a fine product, she might branch out into other commodities, such as sauerkrauts and relishes, attaining, finally, a nationwide clientele under the name of Mrs. Gamp's Particular Pickling Works, or other name, if a better one could be found. I parted company with Mrs. Gamp, who, reflecting on my suggestions, seemed about to go into her kitchen directly and start pickling away.

Day the Ninth

*I*n the morning, having slept in an abandoned chicken coop, not an ideal place to spend an extended time, on the road to Folkestone, I saw sitting beneath a tree where the shade was deepest, a broad, round-shouldered, one-sided old fellow, comically dressed in a pea-overcoat and carrying a large stick. He wore thick shoes, and thick leather gaiters, and thick gloves like a hedger's. Both as to his dress and himself he was of an overlapping rhinoceros build, with folds in his cheeks, and his forehead, and his eyelashes, and his lips, and his ears; but with bright, eager, childishly-inquiring grey eyes under his ragged eyebrows; and a broad-brimmed hat. Altogether a very odd-looking fellow. When I greeted him with my customary "Halloa," he said:

"Morning, Sir; morning, morning."

I remarked, rather unfeelingly I am sorry to say, that he appeared to have fallen on hard times, just as I had, in a way. His story, narrated in a slow, deliberate manner, was as follows:

"Sir, I have the misfortune of being a fool. From a very early age I have detected things those about me thought they hid from me. If I could have been habitually imposed upon, instead of habitually discerning the truth, I might have lived as smoothly as most fools do. My childhood was passed with a grand-mother; that is to say, with a lady who represented that relative to me, and who took that title herself. She had no claim to it, but I—being to that extent a little fool—had no suspicion of her. She had some children of her own family in the house, and some children of other people. All girls; ten in number, including me. We all lived together and were educated together.

"I must have been about twelve years old when I began to see how determinedly those girls patronized me. I was told I was an orphan. I perceived that they conciliated me with an insolent pity, and in a sense of superiority. One of them was my chosen friend. I loved that stupid mite in a passionate way that she could no more deserve, than I can remember without feeling ashamed of, though I was but a child. She had what they call an amiable temper, an affectionate temper. I believe there was not a soul in the place, except myself, who did not know that she purposely wounded and galled me! Nevertheless, I so loved that unworthy girl, that my life was made stormy by my fondness for her. However, I loved her faithfully; and one time I went home with her for the holidays.

"She was worse at home than she had been at school. She tormented my love for her beyond endurance. Her plan was to drive me wild with jealousy. When we were alone, I would reproach her with my perfect knowledge of her baseness, and then she would cry and cry and say I was cruel. And then I would love her as much as ever; often feeling as if I could so hold her in my arms and plunge to the bottom of a river, where I would still hold her, after we were both dead. So ends the sad story of my youth, from which I have never recovered; and so you see me as I am, a pitiable, forsaken old man."

His pathetic story remained in my thoughts for hours after we had parted; and that night I lay in an abandoned carriage, musing on how love can raise one to the clouds or trample one down into the mire; and could not help wondering if I, too, would ever come to such a pass.

Day the Tenth

When I resumed my journey toward Hythe, I gained a little wooden bridge, which, thrown across a stream, led into a meadow where I discerned an encampment of gypsies. These swarthy people, who spend their lives on the open road, living from day to day and hand to mouth, buying and selling horses when they can, and stealing them more often than not, have their own strange ancient ways, and care nothing for the ways of the world.

There were women and children in the camp, going about their tasks of cooking and tending the horses, while the men hung about as if disdainful of such things. A tall athletic man stood with his arms folded, leaning against a tree, smoking a black pipe, which he held in his even blacker teeth, and looking at all the world with a benign malevolence, as though he would just as soon cut your throat as say good morning. Thus it was that I approached the gypsy camp cautiously and with a wary eye open for escape routes.

When I greeted the gypsies with my customary "Halloa," and asked if I might have a cup of water from their buckets, I was told to help myself by the man who leaned against the tree, as follows:

"You were in a mighty hurry a minute ago. Drink if you must, and then be off with you. We suffer no strangers about."

"Don't vex him," pleaded one of the gypsy women, who seemed to be kindlier disposed to strangers.

"Ours is a hard life," said the man who leaned against the tree, who seemed to pay no heed to the woman. "Here to-day, gone to-morrow; the dogs set on us if we pass through a village; not one man showin' us a ounce o' Christian charity. Even little girls are against us because of our ways. I don't deny we have a hearty disdain o' reg'lar work, but what of it? Most men do, though they don't admit it. We're no worse than many others, when you come down to it. I tried bein' a soljer, but it was a hard life, with all them bullets buzzin' about. I tried bein' a sailor, but those cannonballs came conspicuous close. There's too much or too little o' ever'thin' in this old world, and that's the end of it. What do ye think o' that?"

As everyone was looking at me as if I was expected to answer his question, I responded as well as I could, saying that I had never been a soldier or a sailor, but from my own experiences I agreed that there was too much or too little of everything, and it was a lop-sided world, indeed. This seemed to go down well with the entire encampment, and I thought I heard sounds of approval coming from some of the gypsies, even though I didn't understand a word of their strange language.

All of a sudden the gypsies started to dance as if they didn't have a care in the world. First, there was the dance of the gypsy children; then came the dance of the young gypsy men and women; then the dance of the old gypsy men and women. Their music was played on flutes, tambourines, and strange instruments that resembled lutes or guitars, but had more twang to them. It was not unpleasant music, but I supposed it was an acquired taste. Anyhow, the gypsies seemed to enjoy it, and that's all that matters.

I determined, by making myself as agreeable as possible, to stay with the gypsies as long as possible, and try to learn some of their language. It was difficult, however, to take down what I heard in shorthand as none of the marks used in shorthand corresponded to the rather guttural sounds to be heard in their speech. I did learn, however, that these people didn't call themselves gypsies, but Romany. A man is a rye, and a woman is a gitana. Their dress is as colourful as their language, and I thought it would be of interest to the public to learn more about these people, so determined to write a book about them one day.

The gypsies invited me to partake of their evening meal, which was bubbling away in a big iron kettle, and smelled as though a couple of weasels were being cooked in it. I accepted their invitation, of course, but had no idea how I would bring myself to eat such an odouriferous delicacy. I vowed inwardly to avoid grimacing or otherwise showing my reluctance to swallow these creatures, deeming it a small price to pay for an opportunity to observe the gypsies "at home," as it were; their manners, dress, customs, and so forth, an opportunity that might never happen again.

The gypsies showed me how they made their colourful costumes from the bolts of cloth stolen from a draper's shop; how they made their shoes from leather stolen from a tannery; how they constructed their caravans from wood stolen from a lumber-dealer's yard; how they made hinges and hooks and knives from iron stolen from an ironmonger's warehouse; and so forth. They wanted nothing, in short, that could not be stolen from somewhere. I remarked favourably on their inventiveness, which seemed to please them.

Then, too, I learned they were all pick-pockets, having been trained from the cradle, as it were, to live by pilfering instead of paying, which was their credo. They were also expert at bartering with the simple country folk when the opportunity to steal didn't present itself. As to stealing a horse in one village and selling it in the next, before the news was broadcast that a horse was stolen, no one could beat them.

That night I slept in the gypsy encampment, under one of their caravans, as I didn't dare let myself into one of them, they were so dark and dirty inside, where one could easily have one's throat cut. I slept with one eye open, I confess, among people whose humour was not to be depended upon. After a breakfast of I know not what, I made my farewells to the gypsies, who weren't so bad after all, and who simply wanted to live their ways in peace, by their own lights, as they put it.

Day the Eleventh

Next morning there was fog everywhere. Fog up the river, where it flows among green meadows; fog down the river, where it flows among the tiers of shipping; fog on the Kentish marshes and heights; fog creeping into the cabooses of colliers; fog lying out on the yards, and hovering in the rigging of great ships; fog drooping on the gunwales of barges and small boats; fog in the eyes and throats of the old, wheezing by their firesides; fog cruelly pinching the toes and fingers of apprentices; fog everywhere, giving every tree a haggard, drooping look. In a word, FOG!

I learned that there was a fugitive convict, Magwitch by name, on the marshes that very day, as the fog had presented him with an opportunity to effect his escape from the hulks, those dreadful prison-ships, where our fellow human beings are kept under the most appalling conditions. Many men are sent there for crimes no worse than stealing a loaf of bread for their hungry children. Perhaps I will be able, through my writings, to

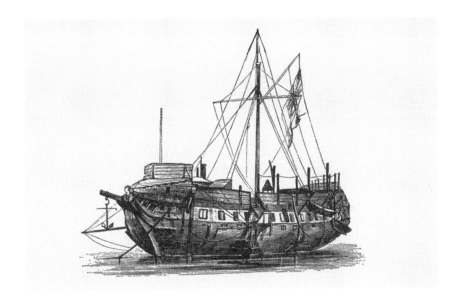

alleviate the condition of such unfortunate creatures, and the poor who live in cities in wretched hovels no better than the hulks themselves. I recall hearing the distant boom of a ship's cannon, signalling, no doubt, that the desperate fellow was being returned to his captivity.

The fog lifted, of course, eventually, and revealed a cloudless sky, most agreeable and welcome after a morning of nothing more, or less, than fog! The blue of the sky was dazzling to the eye in direct proportion to the fog that blinded the eye and rendered it useless for taking one step forward. Thus, the morning was lost, though I was determined to make up for the loss that very afternoon.

Some distance from the road I noticed a house on a hill. It was a very bleak house. The windows were crumbling, and many panes of glass were broken or missing entirely; the door hung on hinges that squeaked like sea-gulls; bricks had fallen out from the walls till the walls resembled toothless old men and women; the path leading to the house was overgrown with weeds of such extraordinary profusion that it would have required a botanist to identify them all. As my own learning in that science amounts to nearly nothing, I will not attempt to describe them, except to say they *were* weeds, and no doubt about it. Between Hythe and Ashford, it was a bleak house, indeed.

The very decrepitude of the place seemed to draw my steps reluctantly toward it. On the door was a rusty knocker on which was engraved a grotesque face, and the name Skimpole. A slatternly, full-blown girl, who seemed to be bursting out of the rents in her dress, and with cracks in her shoes, answered my knock by opening the door as little as possible, and stopping up the gap with her shoe, asked, "What name?" To which I responded appropriately, to which she said, "Quite right."

She led me up the stairs to the first floor, to a room that was dingy enough, and not at all clean, but was furnished with an odd kind of shabby luxury; a large foot-stool and a sofa, and plenty of cushions, an easy-chair, plenty of pillows, a piano, books, drawing materials, music, newspapers, and a few pictures by minor artists. A broken pane of glass in one of the dirty windows was papered and wafered over; but there was a little plate of hothouse peaches on the table, and there was another of grapes, and another of sponge-cakes, and there was a bottle of light wine.

A gentleman reclined on the sofa in a dressing-gown, drinking some fragrant coffee from an old China cup, and looking at the flowers on the balcony. It was then about mid-day. He was not in the least disconcerted by my appearance, but greeted me from his recumbent posture, in an airy manner, as though we were old acquaintances, with the following languid discourse:

"Here I am, you see! Here I am! This is my frugal breakfast. Some men want legs of beef and mutton for breakfast; I don't. Give me my peach, my cup of coffee, and my claret, and I am content. I don't want them for themselves, but they remind me of the Sun. There's nothing solar about legs of beef and mutton. Mere animal satisfaction! Don't you say so?"

As a stranger in his house, I could not but agree. The peaches and the coffee were very inviting, and I hoped the gentleman would prove to be generous to strangers. However, he left me staring at those delicacies, so near and yet so distant, and continued his speech:

"This is the bird's cage [as if unaware of my presence]. This is where the bird lives and sings. I pluck his feathers now and then, and clip his wings; but he sings, he sings!"

This statement he made with a disarming frankness and felicity of expression.

"It is pleasant [said he, looking up at the ceiling] and it is whimsically interesting to trace peculiarities in families, is it not? [I was inclined to answer this question, but realized it was only a rhetorical one.] In this family [limply thrusting his arm outward], we are all children, and I am the youngest [bringing his arm back]. It will sound very strange [no stranger than anything he said thus far, I thought], but we know nothing about chops in this house [I didn't doubt it]. We can't cook anything whatever. A needle and thread we don't know how to use [didn't doubt that, either]. We admire the people who possess the practical wisdom we want, but we don't quarrel with 'em. 'Live and let live,' we say. We have sympathy for everything, have we not?"

As an unbidden guest in the house, I was, of course, in complete agreement with what he said.

"This is a day [said Mr. Skimpole, for that was the recumbent gentleman's name] that will ever be remembered here [I would never forget it, either]. We shall call it St. Clare and St. Summerson Day. You must see my daughters. I have a blue-eyed daughter, who is my Beauty daughter; I have a Sentiment daughter; and I have a Comedy daughter. You must see them all [yes, I was sure I must]. They'll be enchanted [so would I, doubtless]. Time is no object here [surely not]. We never know what o'clock it is, and we never care. Not the way to get on in life, you'll tell me. Certainly. But we *don't* get on in life. We don't pre-*tend* to do it."

Mr. Skimpole left the room and soon came back, bringing with him three young ladies, and Mrs. Skimpole, who had once been a beauty, but was now a delicate high-nosed invalid, suffering patiently under a variety of vexatious complaints.

"This [said Mr. Skimpole, pushing his daughters to the center of the room] is my Beauty daughter, Arethusa—plays and sings and ends like her father; this is my Sentiment daughter, Laura—plays a little, but don't sing; and this is my Comedy daughter, Kitty—sings a little, but don't play. We all draw a little, and compose a little, and none of us have any idea of time or money. It is pleasant and it is whimsically interesting to trace peculiarities in families, don't you think? In this family, we are all children, and *I* am the youngest."

The three daughters were in unanimous agreement. Mr. Skimpole addressed Mrs. Skimpole:

"My dear, it is true, is it not [Mrs. Skimpole could not but agree with Mr. Skimpole]? So it is, and so it must be, because, like the dogs in the hymn, it is our nature to."

The three young Misses Skimpole then performed and sang at the piano, each according to her abilities, which, I confess, didn't amount to much. They sang old Irish melodies and Scottish ballads, with an affectation of suitable native accents that made me wish they hadn't done so, as I fear their ingenuous renditions have ruined that class of

song for me forever. However, Mr. and Mrs. Skimpole enjoyed the performance greatly, out of parental affection, I didn't doubt, which is as it should be.

It was now time to bid farewell to Mr. and Mrs. Skimpole, and the Misses Skimpole, to whom, I confess, I was falsely effusive in my praises of their several talents. Mr. Skimpole was once more reclining on the sofa, eating peaches, not one of which was offered to me during the whole time I was there. As I was leaving this bleak house, I could hear the Misses Skimpole blithely singing away, with not a care in the world.

Day the Twelfth

On the next morning I stopped to rest in a doorway in the village of Ashford. An old man and a young girl were close by. As I squeezed myself tightly into the doorway, I could not help hearing their conversation, when they stopped nearby, which was as follows:

"We must sleep in the open air tonight, grand-father," said the child in a weak voice, "and to-morrow we will beg our way to some quiet part of the country, and try to earn our bread in very humble work."

"Why did you bring me here?" returned the old man fiercely. "I cannot bear these close eternal streets. We came from a quiet part. Why did you force me to leave it?"

"Because I have had that dream I told you of," answered the girl, "and we must live among poor people or it will come again. Dear grand-father, you are old and weak, I know, but look at me. I never will complain if you will not, but I have some suffering, indeed."

"Ah, poor homeless, wandering Nell," cried the old man, clasping his hands and gazing as if for the first time on her anxious face, her

travel-stained dress, her bruised and swollen feet; "has all my agony of care brought you at last to this? Was I a happy man, once, and have I lost happiness and all I had, for this?"

"If we were in the country now," said the child, with assumed cheerfulness, as they looked about for a shelter, "we should find some good old tree, stretching out his green arms as if he loved us, and nodding and rustling as if he would have us fall asleep. Please God, we shall be there soon, tomorrow or next day at the farthest, and in the meantime let us think, dear grand-father, that it was a good thing we came here; for we are lost in the crowd and hurry of this place; and if the cruel Mr. Quilp should pursue us, he never could trace us further. There's comfort in that! And here's a deep old doorway—very dark, but quite dry, and warm, too, for the wind don't blow in here. Who's that?"

Uttering a half-shriek, she recoiled from a black figure, which came suddenly out of the dark recess in which they were about to take refuge. There was a lamp at no great distance; the only one in the place, which was a kind of square yard, but sufficient to show how poor and mean it was. The form was that of a man miserably clad and begrimed with smoke, which, perhaps by its contrast with the natural colour of his skin, made him look paler than he really was. That he was naturally of a wan and pallid aspect, however, his hollow cheeks, sharp features, and sunken eyes, no less than a certain look of patient endurance, sufficiently testified. His voice was harsh by nature, but not brutal. His face, in addition to possessing the characteristics already mentioned, and overshadowed by a quantity of long hair, was neither ferocious nor bad in expression.

"How came you to think of resting here?" he said. "Or how," he added, looking more attentively at the child, "do you come to want a place of rest at this time of day?"

"Our misfortunes are the cause," said the old man.

"Do you know," said the black man, still looking earnestly at the little girl, Nell, "how wet she is, and that the damp streets are not a place for her?"

"I know it well, God help me," said the old grand-father. "What can I do?"

The black man looked at Nell again, and gently touched her garments, from which the rain that had started falling ran off in streams. "I can give you warmth, nothing else. Such lodgings as I have, is in that house, but she is safer and better there than here. The fire is in a rough place, but you can pass the night beside it safely, if you'll trust yourselves to me. You see that red light yonder? It's not far. Shall I take you there? You were going to sleep upon cold bricks; I can give you a bed of warm ashes, nothing better."

Without waiting for any further reply than he saw in their faces, he took Nell in his arms, and bade the old man follow.

That was the last I ever saw or heard of little Nell and her grand-father, whose pathetic tale I have entered in my Journal, with perfect accuracy and, I think, pathos, charm, and some felicity of expression.

I encountered no more remarkable adventures on the road for the remainder of the day; except for meeting a lad with a brimless hat, who was eating gooseberries in the grass, and who carried a small box on his shoulder, in which were deposited, probably, his school-room books and pencils, and perhaps a broken pen-knife to sharpen those pencils. He was doubtless playing the truant, as the school-bell had long since ceased ringing when I saw him, the gooseberries proving, doubtless, more edifying than his school-books. The sight of this untutored boy filled me with great expectations of further picturesque observations, if he was any example.

New adventures were not long in making their appearance. Quite unexpectedly, I came upon two men who were seated in easy attitudes upon the grass, and very busily engaged with repairing some of their equipment. It was not difficult to divine their profession—that of

itinerant showmen, exhibitors of the freaks of Punch; for, perched cross-legged upon a tombstone behind them, was a figure of that droll fellow himself. His nose and his chin were as hooked, and his face as beaming, as usual. Perhaps his imperturbable character was never more strikingly developed, for he preserved his usual equable smile notwithstanding that his body was dangling in a most uncomfortable position, all loose and limp and shapeless; while his long-peaked cap, unbalanced against his exceedingly slight legs, threatened every instant to bring him toppling down.

Scattered upon the ground at the feet of the two men, and jumbled together in a long flat box, were the other persons of the drama: the hero's wife, Judy; the Hobby-horse; the Doctor; the Devil; and the organ were all there. Their owners had evidently stopped at that spot to make some necessary repairs in the stage arrangements; for one of them was engaged in binding together a small gallows with thread, while the other was intent upon fixing a new black wig, with the aid of a small hammer and some brass tacks.

They raised their eyes when I was close upon them, and pausing in their work, returned my greeting with looks of curiosity. One of them, the actual exhibitor, no doubt, was a little merry-faced man with a twinkling eye and a red nose. The other—he that took the money at their performances—had rather a careful and cautious look, which was inseparable from his occupation, also. The merry man was the first to greet me with a nod and a twinkle in his eye, while I observed that it was perhaps the first time I had ever seen a Punch off the stage. Punch, I may add, seemed to be pointing with the tip of his cap to a most flourishing epitaph on the stone, and to be chuckling over it with all his heart.

When I enquired what they might be doing there, the merry man answered:

"Why, you see, we're putting up for tonight at the public-house yonder, and it wouldn't do to let 'em see the present company undergoing repair, because it would destroy all the illusion and take away all the interest, wouldn't it? Would you care a ha'penny for the Lord Chancellor if you know'd him in private, and without his wig on? Certainly not!"

The other man, who had a surly grumbling manner, replied as he twitched Punch off the tombstone, and flung him into a bag:

"You're too free. If you stood in front of the curtain and saw the public faces as I do, you'd know human natur' better."

"Ah," replied the merry man, "it's been the spoilin' of you, Tommy, yer talkin' to that branch. When you played the ghost in the reg'lar dramas in the fairs, you b'lieved in everythin'—except ghosts theirselves. But now ye're a universal mistruster. I never seen a man so changed."

The merry man turned his attention to me, and said:

"If ye're wantin' a place to stop at, I should advise you to take up at the same house with us. That's it, the long, low white house, there. It's very cheap."

I agreed that the house probably was cheap, from the look of it; but as I was counting every farthing in my pockets, and as I could do very well with a haystack, I declined the offer, without offending their sense of taste.

"Look here," said the merry man, "here's all this Judy's clothes fallin' to pieces again. You haven't got a needle and thread, I suppose?"

I answered that I did not, explaining that I carried very little in my knapsack, aside from a change of linen and volumes of Shakespeare and Scott, and that the extra weight of needles and thread might just make it too heavy to support.

"Ah, Shakespeare," said the merry man. "Played Falstaff once, I did. Fell out with the manager, though, and the public, too, when I think of it. There was nothin' left for me in the theatrical way, but this 'ere Punch and Judy, as you can see for yerself. It an't been a bad life, though. Of course, you learn quick enough to live on small rations, but that's all right. We get along."

When I said good-bye to the two theatrical gentlemen, I silently said the same to Punch and Judy, whom I looked upon as old friends.

Day the Thirteenth

The next day started with brilliant sunshine, with not a cloud to mar the view. The fields were green and well-tended by the sturdy folk of Kent. How long would this continue, I reflected. As if in answer to my own question, an inner voice said: Railroads shall soon traverse all this country, and with a rattle and a glare the engines and trains shall shoot like a meteor over the wide night-landscape, turning the Moon pale; but, as yet, such things are nonexistent in these parts, though not wholly unexpected. Preparations are afoot, measurements are made, ground is staked out. Bridges are begun, their not yet united piers desolately look at one another over roads and streams, like brick-and-mortar couples with an obstacle to their union; fragments of embankments are thrown up; everything looks chaotic and in full hopelessness. Along the roads and through the night, the post-chaise makes its way, without a railroad on its mind.

To the side of the road I saw a beautiful little cottage with a thatched roof and little spires at the gable-ends, and pieces of stained glass in some of the windows, almost as large as pocket-books. On one side of the house was a little stable, just the size for a pony. White curtains were fluttering, and birds in cages that looked as bright as if they were made of gold, were singing at the windows; plants were arranged on either side of the path, and clustered about the door; and the garden was bright with flowers in

full bloom, which shed a sweet odour all round, and had a charming and elegant appearance.

Through the door of the cottage was such a kitchen as never was before seen or heard of out of a toy-shop window, with everything in it as bright and glowing, and as precisely ordered, too, as one could wish. And in this kitchen was a table with a white table-cloth, with a knife and a fork, and a dish of cold meat, and pickles, and a beaker of small ale, which could not but fill the fortunate viewer with ardent admiration.

Just outside the city of Canterbury was a blacksmith's forge, with a sign above the door, proclaiming to all the world in rustic letters, that the blacksmith within was one Joe Gargery. From it there issued a tinkling sound, so merry and good-humoured, that it suggested the idea of someone working blithely, and made quite pleasant music. No man who hammered on at a dull monotonous duty could have brought such cheerful notes from steel and iron; none but a chirping, healthy, honest-hearted fellow, who made the best of everything, and felt friendly towards everybody, could have done it for an instant. He might have been a coppersmith, and still been musical. If he had not sat in a jolting waggon, full of rods of iron, it seemed as if he would have brought some harmony out of it.

Tink, tink, tink—clear as a silver bell, and audible at every pause of the street's harsher noises, as though it said, "I don't care; nothing puts me out; I am resolved to be happy." Women scolded, children squealled, heavy carts went rumbling by, horrible cries proceeded from the lungs of hawkers; still it struck on again no higher, no lower, no louder, no softer; not thrusting itself on people's notice a bit the more for having been outdone by louder sounds—tink, tink, tink, tink, tink.

Who but a blacksmith could have made such music? A gleam of sun shining through the unsashed window, and chequering the dark work-shop with a broad patch of light, fell upon him as though attracted by his sunny heart. There he stood working at his anvil, his face all radiant with exercise and gladness, his sleeves turned up, his hair pushed back from his shining forehead—the easiest, freest, happiest man in all the world. Beside him sat a cat, purring and winking in the light, and falling now and then into an idle doze, as from excess of comfort.

As was my custom, I greeted the blacksmith with a hearty "Halloa," and asked how it went with blacksmiths that fine morning. The honest fellow replied:

"It goes very well, young Sir. It's as good a profession as any, see? Just take this 'orseshoe I'm makin' this very minute. Best 'orseshoes as ever was. Why, 'alf the 'orses in the county 'd be lame if it wasn't for me. When I shoes a 'orse, it stays shoed. The doctor's 'orse wants shoein' more 'n any other 'orse in the village, with all the travellin' 'e does, bringin' out babies and calfs, and givin' med'cines to them as is ailin' or dyin'. 'is 'orse wants new shoes every fortnight, see?"

He paused in his discourse for a moment or two, to strike a few blows on the horseshoe under discussion:

"Then there's all these pots and pans wot gets dented when they're throwed by wifes at 'usbands who leave their wages at the Adam and Eve. I bang them dents out proper, till the pots and pans is good as new, ready for the next time to get throwed. There's plenty o' work in that line, see?"

His narration of the life of a blacksmith was indeed worthy of tran-scription, and I enter it in my Journal as faithfully as possible, with the full approval of Mr. Gargery, who seemed mightily pleased to think that his words might appear in a book, some day. He continued his discourse:

"P'rhaps you've a mind to be a smith yourself, eh? Just now, I've need of a 'prentice. You look strong enough for it. The wages an't much, but the work's honest, and you'll sleep o' nights knowin' that you're fair 'n' square with all men. How say you to that, eh?"

I protested that I was more interested in writing about such things than actually doing them, at the moment; but that if ever I decided to become a blacksmith, I would want a man such as himself for a master, at which he seemed highly pleased.

"If you're lookin' to write about things," said Mr. Gargery, "just look around you. See this old 'ammer o' mine? Made it myself when I was a 'prentice, just about your age, I should think. The 'andle's made o' good English oak, and the 'ead's forged out o' Sheffield steel. Been usin' this very 'ammer thirty year and more, and it's good for an 'undred more after I go to *my* Maker. This old leathern apron has withstood more sparks than the Devil 'imself could throw at it. I'd be scorched all over, if it wasn't for this apron, see?"

A few more blows to the anvil, then:

"Just look around you. See them old tools 'angin' on the walls? If they could talk, wot larks they'd tell. Take that winder over there; glass is broke, sure, but the Sun comes shinin' through it every mornin', none the worse for that. Every mornin' that same old Sun warms my 'eart and makes me thankful to see it again."

I could not help but agree that his shop was an admirable place, and it made my heart glad to see it, and him happily working away in it. I would not forget it or him soon, I promised, as I took my leave of Mr. Joe Gargery, who was as proud of being a blacksmith as any man ever was proud of his own profession. The sound of his hammer striking the anvil followed me, as I continued my way through the village, until it faded away finally... tink, tink, tink.

I had not walked far when I saw an old man leaning against a gate at the side of the road. This was a man with dirty feet and garments, who stood bareheaded; and when he turned his face upward toward me, the brightness of the Sun told me he was blind. I greeted him with my customary "Halloa," to which he responded cheerfully:

"A blessing on your voice! Will you speak more, and cheer the heart of a traveller?"

I asked if he had no guide, as he was alone and carried only a staff to lead him on over field and road.

"None but that," he answered, pointing with his staff toward the Sun.

I asked if he had travelled far.

"A weary and a long way," rejoined the blind man, for such he was, as he shook his head, "a weary, weary way, Sir. Alas, I see nothing, waking *or* sleeping—nothing. But my senses are alert and I see more than men think I see. Use and necessity are good teachers, as I have learned—the best of any. May you never learn under them. They are rough masters."

I offered him a drink from a nearby brook, and bread from my knapsack. He raised the cup of water to his mouth. It was clear, and cold, and sparkling, but he only wetted his lips and put the cup down and thanked me for my kindness. When I asked if it was hard, being a blind man, he answered:

"There are various degrees and kinds of blindness, Sir. There is the connubial blindness, which is a kind of willful and self-bandaging blindness. There is the blindness of party, and public men, which is the blindness of a mad bull in the midst of a regiment of soldiers clothed in red. There is the blind confidence of youth—begging your pardon, Sir—which is the blindness of young kittens, whose eyes have not yet opened on the world; and there is that physical blindness, of which I am, contrary to my desire, a most illustrious example. Added to these, is that blindness of the intellect, of which the world has so many outstanding specimens. So you see, Sir, being blind in *my* way an't half as bad as being blind in those *other* ways. My name is Smike; what, pray, is yours?"

Having delivered himself of this vehement discourse, with many flourishes of his staff, Mr. Smike drew from beneath his coat a flat stone bottle; and pulling the cork with his teeth, proceeded to quench his thirst with an infusion of its contents, smacking his lips with infinite relish. With his words still fresh in my mind, the blind man and I parted company, he going his way, I going mine. I consoled myself that I was not suffering from any of the blindnesses he had mentioned—at least, not yet.

Day the Fourteenth

Closer still to the city of Canterbury, on this fourteenth day of my journey, I saw a small church, a structure of wood shingles painted white, that had begun to flake off for want of attention. Before the church was a graveyard, the oldest grave not more still and quiet than the churchyard itself. The cold hoar-frost glistened on the tombstones and sparkled like rows of gems. It seemed as if corpses, hidden only by their winding sheets, were as quiet as the stones on which their names were engraved.

I opened the church door and entered, and was refreshed immediately by the coolness within. A verger was, at the moment, busily sweeping out the aisle of a few stray leaves, and tending to his other duties in the edifice. As we were in a sacred place, I refrained from shouting "Halloa," but greeted him in a more subdued tone. He seemed to welcome a visitor in the lonely church, when, all of a sudden, a young girl entered the church, crying out:

"Father, father!"

The verger heard the voice of the girl and greeted her. She had bright eyes, indeed—eyes that would bear a world of looking into before their depth was fathomed. Dark eyes, that reflected back the eyes that searched them, namely, mine—eyes that were beautiful and true, and beaming

with hope. The verger kissed the young girl, who just happened to be his daughter, and who just happened to be bringing him his supper in a basket. She said:

"Smell it, dear father! Only smell it!"

The verger took the shortest possible sniff at the edge of the basket, and then cried out in rapture:

"Why, it's hot!"

"It's burning hot," replied the girl. "Ha, ha, ha—it's scalding hot!"

"Ha, ha, ha," said the verger, with a kick of satisfaction. "It's scalding hot!"

He then proceeded to question his daughter in a rather playful way, as though she were still a six-year-old child:

"It an't, I suppose, it an't polonies?"

His daughter said it wasn't polonies.

"It an't, I suppose, it an't trotters?" said the verger.

His daughter said it wasn't trotters.

"It an't, I suppose, it an't sausages?" said the verger.

His daughter said it wasn't sausages.

"It an't, I suppose, it an't tripe?" said the verger.

"It *is* tripe!" said his daughter, who was as delighted as a six-year-old to play the game.

"Tripe!" cried the verger in a paroxysm of joy. "Hot tripe! Lovely tripe! Tripe o' my heart! It an't, I suppose, it an't peppered?"

His daughter said it *was* peppered.

"It an't, I suppose, it an't salted?" said the verger.

His daughter said it *was* salted.

After taking but one taste of the tripe that was still hot and bubbling

"This is the best tripe as ever was, and you're the best daughter as ever was, and no mistake on both scores."

The verger sat down on the steps of the church and ate his supper with relish, smacking his lips and clicking his busy tongue after each bite. And he did justice to the potatoes, too, that accompanied the tripe, as though they knew they were in good company. I could not help wishing, from the steam that assaulted my nose, that there was another spoon in that basket.

"He'd eat his supper with an appetite, wherever he was," said the young girl, whose name was Meg (as the verger called her), and whose eyes pierced through mine.

Once the verger finished his supper, which was dispatched in a more lively manner than I had ever seen before, he quieted down and in an expansive mood, related the following story:

"It was a cold and blustery night. The wind was so strong, that it was as much as I could do to shut the church door, by putting my whole weight against it; and even as it was, it burst wide open twice, with such strength that you would have sworn, if *you* had been leaning against it, that somebody was pushing on the other side. However, I got the key turned, went into the belfry, and wound up the clock—which was very near run down, and would have stood stock-still in half an hour. As I took up my lantern again to leave the church, it came upon me all at once that it was the nineteenth of March. It came upon me with a kind of shock, as if a hand had struck the thought upon my forehead; at the very same moment, I heard a voice outside the tower—rising from among the graves.

"Never tell me that it was my fancy, or that it was any other sound which I mistook for that I tell you of. I heard the wind whistle through the arches of the church. I heard the steeple strain and creak. I heard the rain as it came driving against the walls. I felt the bells shake. I saw the ropes sway to and fro. And I heard that voice."

He paused to gather his thoughts, and sweep up a few more leaves from the aisle, then continued:

"When I opened the church door to come out," said the verger, his face ample testimony to the sincerity of his conviction, "which I did suddenly, for I wanted to get it shut again before another gust of wind came up, there crossed me, so close that by stretching out my finger I

could have touched it, something in the likeness of a man. It turned its face without stopping, and fixed its eyes on mine. It was a ghost—a spirit! Seated on a tombstone was this strange, unearthly figure, no being of this world. His long, fantastic legs might have reached the ground if they were not cocked up and crossed after a quaint, fantastic fashion; his sinewy arms were bare, and his hands rested on his knees. On his short round body he wore a close covering, ornamented with small slashes; a short cloak dangled at his back, the collar cut into curious peaks, which served him as a neckerchief; and his shoes curled up at the toes in long points. The figure looked as though he had been sitting comfortably on that stone for two or three hundred years. He was grinning as only a spirit could!"

I could not help but cry out whose ghost might it have been. But the verger, once more intent on his sweeping, seemed not to notice my cry or even my presence there. Eventually, he spoke once more, not to me, but rather to the empty church:

"It was the likeness of a murdered man. It was the nineteenth of March. Let us keep it to ourselves, for the present time. That a ghost as has been a man of sense in his lifetime would be out walking in such weather—I only know that *I* wouldn't, if I was one."

As the afternoon was hastening toward evening, the verger climbed to the belfry to ring the hour. The sound of the bells filled the small church until every corner of it resounded to their rise and fall. When he returned, he said his name was Trotty Veck, and he had been the verger for over twenty years. When we parted, I supped from my knapsack, with the smell of the unattainable tripe still fresh in my memory. Among the many curious inscriptions on the tombstones was the following:

HERE INTERR'D GEORGE ANDERSON DOTH LIE
BY FALLEN ON AN ANCHOR HE DID DYE

IN SHEERNESS YARD ON GOOD FRIDAY
YE 6TH OF APRIL, I DO SAY
ALL YOU THAT READ MY ALLEGY: BE ALWAYS
READY FOR TO DYE. AGED 42 YEARS.

I had no sooner left the precincts of the church than I perceived a man approaching me. He was gravely attired, if I may be permitted to use a word so fresh in my mind. As to his coat, it was black; as to his leggings, they were pepper-and-salt; as to his hair, it was touched here and there with grey; as to his whiskers, they were white; as to his smile, it extended beyond the confines of his mouth and was like the snarl of a cat; as to his cravat, it was stiff and white and closely knotted; as to his overall appearance, it was, as I have stated, decidedly *grave*.

When I asked how he did his fine evening, he answered:

"As to that, very well, thank you."

When I asked what his business was there, he answered:

"As to that, it's my own, thank you."

When I asked if he was father to any children, he answered:

"As to that, only my wife knows for certain, thank you."

When I asked his denomination, he answered:

"As to that, it's between myself and the Lord, thank you."

When I asked what his political views were, he answered:

"As to that, I sit on a fence and watch how the wind blows, thank you."

When we parted, as suddenly as we had met, this recalcitrant gentleman said, "Barkus is willin'," which I found to be as enigmatic as anything else he said.

On this, the last day of my journey, I entered the city of Canterbury, and aimed my steps directly to the great cathedral where so much of our history has transpired. I passed through the archway that leads to the cathedral grounds, with its beautiful gardens filled with fragrant flowers, and its well-kept paths and smooth turf, as though an army of gardeners considered it their great honour to keep it so. How beautiful the cathedral was, that soared heavenward, with its old stone balustrades and parapets, and wide flights of shallow steps, seamed by time and weather; and how the trained ivy grew up the walls as though the garden would be content only if it could embrace the beloved cathedral; and dark windows diversified by

turreted towers and porches of eccentric design, where old stone lions and gargoyles leered from their heights at the puny mortals below. The chimes of the cathedral just then began to fill the air with sacred music, and I could not help thinking they were ringing a welcome to me.

Thence, the path wound underneath a gateway, through a courtyard where the principal entrance was. I entered the cathedral and walked into the chapel where Becket was murdered by the king's men and martyred. It was a place of veneration where pilgrims left flowers on the steps of the small altar. The air was cool and sweet with the smell of candles and incense, and the muffled steps of the pilgrims went softly through the aisles, while their eyes swept heavenward to the ceiling, so high from where they stood as to seem as though it was in another realm.

The cathedral organist, practicing his art on the great organ of hundreds of pipes, filled the edifice with the divine music of the masters. It was difficult to suppress a tear at the sound of the instrument, which seemed to presage the music of heaven itself. Priests came through the great aisle, on their way to Evensong, greeted by the bows and genuflections of the visitors. The great stained-glass windows, in their beautiful sombre colour, added to the solemn effect of the music that swelled through the cathedral.

I rested on a stone bench in one of the cloisters and meditated, while two novices read their breviaries. The silence of the cathedral and the

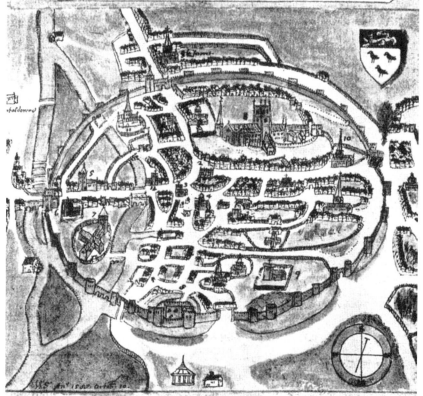

CANTERBVRY.

1. Chriſts church.
2. ŷ market Place.
3. our Lady.
4. St. Andrewes.

5. St. Peter.
6. weſtgate church.
7. St. mildred.
8. The Caſtell.

9. our Lady.
10. St. george.
11. The freeres.
12. Alhalores.

cloister was the silence one might find on a desert island, far from the routes of shipping, with only the whisper of the trade winds to intrude on the ear. For the moments I sat there, I felt as though I *were* on a desert island, with my own thoughts for company. The novices walked past my bench, and, deep in prayer, scarcely noticed my presence. I would have liked to engage them in conversation, but refrained from speaking, as they might have been sworn to a life of contemplative silence. A bubbling fountain of old stone-work in the center of the cloister was the only rude sound that intruded on the profound peace I felt there.

I thought there was no finer place to end one's journey than in a great cathedral, where many have found their journey's end; but where, I was certain, *my* journey had only just begun.

Illustrations

Page 2: Portraits of Hablot Knight Browne ("Phiz") and George Cruikshank. 3: Sample of Dickens's handwriting. 4: Title page by George Cruikshank. 5: Covers for foreign translations. 7: The Pilgrims' Way from London. 11: Dickens at eighteen, from a miniature by his aunt Janet Barrow. 12: Warrens' Blacking Warehouse, Hungerford Stairs. 13: Boy labeling pots of blacking-paste. 14: Marshalsea debtors' prison and seated inmate by Frederick Barnard. 15: Illustration by George Cruikshank. 17: Sample of Dickens's shorthand. 18: Top, illustration by Richard Doyle; bottom, Half Moon tap by Isaac Robert Cruikshank. 19: Illustration from The English Illustrated Magazine, 1884. 23: Illustration by Richard Doyle. 24: Illustration by Frederick Barnard. 29: Illustration by Phiz. 31: Theater poster with Dickens's name listed. 32: Dickens in Every Man in His Humour, painting by C.R. Leslie; in Used Up, painting by Augustus Egg. 35: Illustration by Phiz. 37: Illustration by Phiz. 39: Etching by George Cuitt. 41: Illustration by A. Morrow. 42: Illustration by Phiz. 44: Illustration by Phiz. 46: Illustration by Clayton Clark ("Kyd"). 47: Illustration by Robert Seymour. 51: Illustration by Phiz. 53: Illustrations by C. Napier Hemy. 56: Illustration by Hemy. 57: Ilustration by Hemy. 58: Illustration by Barnard. 60: Illustration by Barnard. 62: Nineteenth-century actor as Falstaff. 63: Etching by Cuitt. 66: Illustration by Phiz. 67: Illustration by Randolph Caldecott. 69: Illustration by Phiz. 70: Illustration by L.R. O'Brien. 71: Illustration by Barnard. 73: Illustration by Phiz. 77: Illustration by Ernest Waterlow. 79: Illustration by Phiz. 82: Dickens by "Spy." 86: Illustration by Willy Pogany. 87: Illustration by Thomas Hood. 88: London in a November fog. 90: Etching by John Crome. 91: Illustration by J.T. Smith. 92: Dickens by Harry Furniss. 93: Illustration by Hood. 94: Illustration by Thackeray. 96: Illustration by George Cattermole. 97: Illustration by Cattermole. 98: Illustration by Phiz. 99: Illustration by Hood. 100: Illustration by R.W. Macbeth. 101: Illustration by Hemy. 102: Illustration by Barnard. 104: Adam and Eve Tavern, etching by Whistler. 105: Illustration by Barnard. 107: Illustration by Phiz. 108: Illustration by John Leech. 111: Illustration by Phiz. 112: Illustration by Barnard. 116: Map of Canterbury, 1588. 117: Pilgrims of Chaucer's time.

Bibliography

In addition to the works of Charles Dickens, the following works have been consulted in the making of this "Journal":

Cruikshank, R.J. *Charles Dickens and Early Victorian England*. London: Sir Isaac Pitman and Sons, Ltd., 1949.

Forster, John. *The Life of Charles Dickens*. London: Chapman & Hall, Limited; and Humphrey Milford. n.d.

Johnson, Edgar. *Charles Dickens His Triumph and Tragedy*. New York: Simon and Schuster, 1952.

Leacock, Stephen. *Charles Dickens His Life and Work*. Garden City, New York: Doubleday Doran Company, Inc., 1936.

Marcus, Steven. *Dickens: From Pickwick to Dombey*. New York: Basic Books, Inc., 1965.

Marzials, Frank T. *Life of Charles Dickens*. London: Walter Scott, 24 Warwick Lane, Paternoster Row, 1887.